LAST STOP

PAUL LUNDY

Copyright ©2025 Paul Lundy. All rights reserved. Leprechaun Publishing, Inc. published this work in the United States. The author prohibits any reproduction or transmission of this book in any form or by any means without written permission from the author. This work is fiction.

ISBN: 979-8-218-85845-2

Cover art design by Paul Lundy

For my dad, who taught me an inch is a cinch, and a mile takes a while, and for allowing me to stay up late as a child to watch Shock Theatre with him, hosted by Barry "Dr. Creep" Hobart.

Prologue

The ambulance swayed from side to side as Lindsey fought to keep John Doe stable in the back.

"Hey take it easy up there," she said.

"It's the wind," the driver, Harry, said, his knuckles white on the wheel. "I don't get it."

"What don't you get, Harry?" she said.

"It feels like we're caught in a whirlwind, yet the leaves on the trees we're passing are completely still."

A thunderclap interrupted their conversation.

"Wow, that sounded like it exploded right overhead," she said.

"Yeah. Funny thing is, I don't see any lightning," Harry said.

Lindsey glanced through the rear window of the vehicle, anticipating the next thunder but seeing only darkness. The occasional jolts and rattles interrupted the steady hum of the ambulance's engine and the rhythmic beeping of the machine.

"It must be getting ready to let loose," Lindsey said.

"Yeah, no kidding," Harry said, "but be it the evening and the conditions we're experiencing, I'd expect to see blinding lightning slicing across the sky in jagged spikes like plotted values on a graph."

Lindsey felt drawn to the handsome man resting in a coma beside her. Her gaze lingered on his appearance with her eyes brushing over his features much like an artist meticulously critical with painting every detail. She tried to imagine his face without the respirator, thick black hair cascading over his forehead, the smoothness of his clean-shaven jaw.

Any woman wrapped up in his strong embrace and against his broad shoulders would feel safe, she thought.

But then she glanced at his fingernails. She paused for a moment. They were creepy—long and pointed like sharp talons, resembling the claws of a predatory animal more than the hands of a man. A curious thought crossed her mind: had his caregiver played a cruel joke by trimming his nails into such an eerie shape? The contrast between his inviting appeal and the grotesque fingernails left her feeling both intrigued and uneasy. He was like a beautiful rose with hidden thorns.

"Good thing trick-or-treat is over," Lindsey said.

"Yeah. Halloween always brings out the crazies," Harry said.

Lindsey remembered she had a pair of fingernail clippers tucked in her uniform jacket. She had always found various practical uses for them in countless situations, from using the nail file to open letters to cutting fishing line whenever her husband got it snagged on a tree or rock. She had even used them to snip twine while bundling cut ornamental grass or branches from trimming bushes. She retrieved the pair of clippers from her right jacket pocket and attempted to trim John Doe's fingernails.

Meanwhile, Harry's hand reached for the radio, and out of his peripheral vision he saw something unexpected. A young boy clad in a tattered Grim Reaper costume stood in the middle of the street, his presence a sinister omen, both eerie and surreal. Harry's foot instinctively lifted from the accelerator, but it was too late; his heart raced as he watched the boy wind up and hurl an egg toward the windshield. The egg exploded upon impact, showering the glass with a grotesque mess of slime, yellow yolk, and shattered shell fragments that smeared his vision. The boy sidestepped, dodging a close encounter just as Harry swerved to avoid him. Had it not been for Harry, squinting with desperation through the semitransparent mucus-like egg white coating the left of the windshield versus the opaque yellow yolk centered in his view, the outcome could've been grave, a chilling thought that lingered in the air.

"Don't tell me that was the wind," Lindsey said.

She inspected the clippers after struggling to trim John Doe's nails. Despite her efforts, she couldn't make any progress; the arm of the clippers broke, rendering the tool unusable, even for twine. Looking down at his fingernails, she noticed they were unscathed, as if they were indestructible.

Harry activated the windshield wipers, but instead of clearing the view, they only smeared the yolk, making it more difficult for him to see the road ahead.

"See what I mean," Harry said, casting his words over his right shoulder. "We just got egged."

"Just keep it on the road, will you," Lindsey said, half listening to Harry.

Harry slowed to clean the windshield with a couple of spurts of cleaner before moving on.

"Wait a second," Harry said as he turned into a drive-thru.

"What are you doing?" Lindsey said.

"I need to grab a pack of cigarettes and a lottery ticket," Harry said.

"Make it quick, I need to pee," Lindsey said.

He struck the curb, tapping the brakes, causing the vehicle to buck like a wild horse, jerking Lindsey's kidneys with each jarring movement

"That's not funny," Lindsey said.

"Oh, sorry about that," Harry said, finding amusement in the idea of Lindsey tinkling a few drops onto her panties.

As the ambulance entered the drive-thru, it was as if Harry had summoned the fury of the storm to enter. Behind the counter, a gaunt man in a vendor's cap blinked in mute bewilderment. The display racks of Ding Dongs and Hostess cherry pies trembled at first, then rattled in a jittery percussion, the wrappers swelling under the shifting pressure until seams split and cakes burst forth like viscera from a wound. Bags of popcorn and potato chips twitched and then ballooned, the plastic stretching to translucency before erupting in clouds of food fragments. Hard candy, individually wrapped in orange and purple foil, pinwheeled through the air. The pieces ricocheted off the glass doors of the refrigerated cases, each impact sounding a staccato Morse code of calamity. Inside the cases, the bottled sodas and energy drinks reacted with peculiar violence: rows of blue Gatorade and orange Mountain Dew shivered and then detonated, the caps blown off and the fluid arcing in sticky geysers. Before the glass could fog, the doors themselves began to hum and resonate, the vibration building until each cooler was a tuning fork for the madness that had entered. A six-pack of root beer, the cans soldered together by plastic rings, sailed past the vendor's head and burst on the far wall, leaving twin brown trails running down the faded posters of sports teams and bikini models. The man behind the counter grabbed the metal edge of his register and ducked. He tried to say something, but the wind inside the building snatched the words from his lips and sent them sailing out the open door like a riptide carrying away a dead body into the vast nothingness. While in a crouched position, the vendor flinched as the cash register's receipt spool unfurled and whipped about his neck like a paper serpent. A metal rack of beef jerky toppled, its contents torn from the hooks and sent spinning, leathery and wild, in the slipstream. Somewhere in the clamor, a display rack of lighters tumbled to the ground. The fluorescent lights overhead flickered, then failed, plunging the store into a strobe-lit dusk.

Inside the ambulance, Lindsey shifted her gaze away from the chaos outside the backdoor windows and focused once more on John Doe, reflecting on how he was the calm at the center of the storm.

Harry opened his window to talk to the man hiding behind the counter.

"It's not me," he said, feeling the man's frustration directed at him for the cyclone of disarray.

The vendor's furious expression made Harry realize it wasn't the right moment to request a pack of smokes. Especially after reading the overuse of profanity from the vendor's lips. He rolled up the window and sped out of the drive-thru.

Just as the tail end of the ambulance exited the drive-thru, the glass doors of the coolers finally succumbed, shattering outward in a crystalline bloom.

"What was that all about?" Lindsey said.

"I don't know," Harry said, "but I sure could use a cigarette right about now."

"Here," Lindsey said.

She handed Harry a pack of cigarettes.

"You smoke?" Harry said.

"No," Lindsey said. "They came in through the open window."

"My brand," Harry said.

CHAPTER 1

Though his eyes had aged, Jed Myers could still distinguish the section of Bohemian Grove Cemetery lit by solar panel lights on stakes from his vantage point across the street at the Weather the Storm Nursing Home, where he lived. From his wheelchair, he peered through the large picture window at the part of the cemetery that held the most significance for him. The area shrouded in a considerable amount of darkness marked the graves of the children. As dusk fell, the window Jed was looking through, in stark contrast to the lit hallway, reflected a glassy appearance that had seemed transparent just hours earlier. When Kate approached him from behind, she noticed the reflection of Jed's eyes in the glass, confirming that he was aware of her presence.

"You'd think as much time you spend looking at that cemetery by now, you'd find a good spot to be buried in," Kate said.

"Is that what you think I'm doing?" Jed said.

"Well, what else could it be?" Kate said. "At your age, I hope you're not expecting some young girl to see you from the sidewalk and say, 'Hey handsome, where have you been all my life?' Come on. You've been sitting here for hours."

"Up on that cemetery hill, 92 children lay at rest, and I could've saved them," Jed said.

"Wow, you have a lot on your mind," Kate said. "Should I just leave you to wallow in your sorrows? Perhaps I could drop off a box of tissues to you while I attend to more important things. I mean, I would say you need to forget the past and get on with your life but you don't have a life, do you? All you have to hold on to is your history."

"I have one word to say to you and nothing more," Jed said.

"Yeah, and what's that?" Kate said.

"Karma," Jed said.

Kate drew the shades, closing off the outside.

Moments later, Harry could see the sign that said Weather the Storm Nursing Home illuminated by the headlights. The ambulance teetered as it entered the driveway.

"We're here," Harry said.

"Still among the living," Lindsey said in a low voice. "A feat worth mentioning in my daily diary."

As the ambulance backed into position with a low, rumbling growl, a couple of nurses emerging from their 3-11 shift obliged to assist in opening the second set of heavy doors that led out to the covered driveway entrance. The moment the ambulance edged closer to the building, the winds picked up, swirling around them with a fierce intensity, whipping the nurse's hair into a bird's nest. The nurse managing the left door winced as a few strands lashed against her left eye. The sting caught her off guard. The second she felt the pain; she weighed the possibility of having an eye injury while wearing glasses. She prayed she wouldn't receive a corneal abrasion.

Inside the nursing home, the paramedics maneuvered the stretcher with care, wheeling the patient just beyond the outer doors in the west wing, right outside the room of Mrs. Rose

Windslow. A rancid odor, reminiscent of decaying flesh, clung to the walls and hung thick in the air like the residue of cigarette tar in a cheap motel room, the kind that leave their stench embedded in carpets and drapes. One wheel on the stretcher wobbled, discordant and out of sync with the others. Televisions dangled from the ceilings, their volumes too loud for the young nurses, broadcasting game shows, westerns, and the weather reports that echoed through the hallways to the deaf ears of the elderly, sound asleep and unaware of the wayward world outside. They couldn't have cared less whether pizza restaurants used one hundred percent mozzarella cheese, or if the two million acres of land—equivalent to the size of Delaware—designated for golf courses in America could be used to grow more food and provide shelter for the homeless, or if the looming threat of a nuclear attack from Russia was imminent.

Hearing the commotion down the hallway, Kate disengaged from her conversation with Jed, leaving him to his thoughts as she made her way to the nurses' station to meet the paramedics.

Lindsey gave a perfunctory report: "Name unknown, possible head trauma, unresponsive since pickup. File in the folder." She peeled off her gloves and tossed them into the nearest biohazard bin.

Kate eyed the stretcher and the new arrival.

She took the file from Harry, expecting the usual stack—recent labs, medical history, next of kin—but the manila folder was almost empty. She flipped it open and found only a single sheet, with the patient's vital stats and a scribbled "John Doe–Unknown." There was a coffee stain in the upper right corner, and the edges were creased as if someone had used the folder as a coaster.

"This is all you have," Kate said, holding the receiving paper so tight it curved in her hand as if she were constructing a makeshift funnel.

"Sorry to dump this baby off on your doorstep, sweetness," Lindsey said.

"That's just great," Kate said.

"Look, I really need to go," Lindsey said. "If you could point me towards the ladies' room…"

Kate raised her arm, cutting Lindsey's sentence off, and pointed down the hallway. "To the right," she said.

"Thanks," Lindsey said, raising her eyebrows, looking at Harry in disbelief, and then rolling her eyes as she walked away.

"You know, this all seems odd," Harry said in a low voice.

"You're telling me," Kate said. "Just where exactly am I supposed to place him? We're already full."

"I mean, no one knows where he came from or who dropped him off at the hospital," Harry said.

Kate stopped, clipboard in hand, and gave Harry her full attention. "So, what are you saying? You're saying…"

"Yes," he said.

He looked at her, his eyes serious. "I'm saying this guy just… showed up. Out of nowhere."

Kate narrowed her eyes, being skeptical. She searched his eyes for honesty while busying her mind with believing he must believe the story to be true. She let out a thin, disrespectful laugh, but Harry didn't flinch.

"None of the nurses knew he was there," he said, his voice dropping even lower. "One of them—can't remember her name, maybe Angie or

Lisa—went to prep the room and found him already in the bed. Unconscious. No paperwork. No chart. No IVs set. Just him. Lying just as you now see him."

"In a coma?" Kate said.

"Yes," he said, "but that isn't the only thing that stands out as being bizarre."

She pressed the chart to her chest.

"Come on," Kate said. "Someone had to have admitted him. Hospitals don't just let random coma patients stroll in and get comfortable in a bed."

"I'm telling you, that's what happened," Harry insisted. "The charge nurse checked the log. There was no record of anyone bringing him in, but he was there, hooked up to a ventilator. Except—" He paused, voice trembling slightly now, as if the surrounding air had gotten colder. "Except no one in the entire hospital signed off on it."

"Why are you whispering?" Kate said.

He paused, looking toward John Doe, then swallowed.

"None of the respiratory therapists intubated him," Harry said, barely above a whisper.

"That's impossible," Kate said.

"Yeah? Well, there are no orders, no doctor's signature designating him as a candidate for long-term care," he said.

"Look, I know it's Halloween and all, but if you're trying to scare me, it's not working," Kate said. "People cannot put themselves on a ventilator."

He shrugged.

Kate widened her eyes, expressing that he must be crazy. She placed the patient's chart on a clipboard.

Harry reached out, touching her forearm. "There's more," he said.

She braced herself. "Go on," she said.

"After he arrived, things started happening."

"What kind of things?" she said.

"Small stuff, at first. Vitals monitors going haywire. Staff getting nosebleeds. One orderly—a big guy, played football in high school—he fainted just walking past the room. Said he felt a cold rush, like walking through an open freezer. They sent him home early."

Kate felt the electric prickle of goosebumps along her forearms, but she kept her voice steady.

"It's a hospital, Harry. Weird stuff happens. People get freaked out."

"Yeah, but he never came back," Harry said, emphasizing with wide eyes. He started to say something else, but stopped himself. "Just... be careful, okay?"

She shrugged, trying to appear tough. "I'm always careful."

Rose Windslow came awake with a suddenness that nearly stopped her heart. Her eyes snapped open to the blank ceiling above her hospital bed, but the world felt altered from the one she'd known when she'd drifted off just minutes before. She was clutching a threadbare blanket to her chest as protection against the chill that clung to the west wing, burrowing into her old bones. It wasn't the cold alone that made her shudder. No, it was something else—something she couldn't name, an invisible force that had entered her dreams and followed her back to waking life, dripping with purpose.

The dream had started out on a near perfect day. In the dream, she was seven again, standing on a sloping hill on the edge of Bohemian Grove, her mother beside her, both of them laughing as they struggled to keep hold of a homemade kite. The wind was perfect, the sky a wooly patchwork of blue and white, and her mother's voice—long gone in the waking world—was as warm and real as the sun. They'd eaten triangle-shaped sandwiches with the crusts cut off, and for one blessed moment, Rose was back in a body that didn't ache or protest, back in a time before old age and loneliness had hollowed her out.

Her beautiful dream had morphed into an undesirable aura. The once-pink cherry blossom trees, creating a snow of pink petals landing in a circle around the base of the trunks like felt Christmas tree skirts, now appeared lifeless, charred as if a fire had swept through, leaving a somber atmosphere. Her mother was gone, with only her smoldering white shoes remaining and a memory of a hand that had only moments ago clasped hers. The sky, once joyful, turned angry. Dark, heavy clouds amassed above her, and the wind howled, tangling her long copper hair. Rose's kite, a bright triangle soaring against the gray sky, wobbled as the tail, made from her mother's bra, flailed out-of-control. The kite struggled against the gusty wind to stay airborne. She looked around, searching for her mother or anyone at all, but the meadow was now deserted—abandoned in the silence that pressed itself deep into her ears. Then, without warning, a bolt of lightning split the sky and struck the kite dead center. The impact hurled her backwards, and as she tumbled through the air, she saw the kite burning, plummeting toward her like a bird of prey with glowing red eyes. She opened her mouth to scream, but no sound came, only the smell of ozone and singed fabric.

She woke before the kite could hit her, but the smell lingered, acrid and sharp. For a long moment, she lay still, listening to the slow, arrhythmic thump of her heart. She wasn't sure if she was alive or dead. The edges of the dream clung to her, sticky and threatening to pull her back under if she let her guard down for even a second.

That's when she realized she wasn't alone. Not just spiritually—she was used to feeling the presence of her deceased relatives or the occasional phantom visitor—but literally. Something was in the hallway just beyond her door. Not a person, but the contrary, a shape, a dark presence, an immortal abomination. She could feel it in the way her skin prickled up and her mouth went dry. She gripped the blanket tighter, huddling beneath it as if the flimsy cotton could serve as armor against the unknown.

She listened for a moment, filtering the sound of the television set coming from the next room, the faint conversation between a man and woman across the hallway, and the steady hum of the heater just below the window. Beneath all that, a quieter rhythm pulsed—something mechanical. She found it impossible to ignore.

With effort, she propped herself up on one elbow, every joint in her arm creaking in protest. The movement sent a tremor of pain through her shoulder, but she ignored it. Rose had been through worse. She inched herself higher until she could peer through her open door, out into the pale fluorescent glow of the hallway. She saw a gurney parked across from her room, against the far wall in a shadowed pocket of light. It was one of the newer ones, metal rails gleaming and wheels locked precisely in place, but the sight of it filled her with an irrational dread.

On the gurney lay a man, so motionless he might have been carved from marble. His skin was pale, the color of the bedsheets tucked around him, and his hair was coal black. His hands lay at his sides. Even from her distance, Rose could tell he was not asleep. He was in the kind of coma that looked less like rest than a rehearsal for the grave.

Rose stared at the man for a long time, her eyes refusing to blink. She could sense a tension in the room, the kind that builds before a thunderstorm. She knew, with the certainty of someone who had seen too many people die, that the man on the gurney was the source of the dread that had invaded her sleep and now cloaked the hallway. She tried to look away, but found that she couldn't; she was as tethered to his presence as she had been to her burning kite in the dream.

She struggled with how the gurney had gotten there, silent as a ghost, while she slept without even a rouse. Had she been a young adult, she would've heard the commotion, the shuffle of feet while being wheeled into place. She craned her neck, trying to get a better look. She thought she saw a faint movement—a subtle rise and fall of the man's chest—but it might have just been the shadow of the blanket shifting with the air from the vent overhead. She squinted, holding her own breath so she could better sense if he breathed.

She tried to convince herself that it was only the remnants of her nightmare, that the sense of dread was nothing more than a hangover from the lightning strike and her mother leaving her alone. But the more she stared at the gurney, the more convinced she became that she was right to be afraid.

She lay back, her head pressed into the crinkling hospital pillow, and tried to slow her breathing. She listened once again for the sounds of life from the nurses' station, needing to anchor herself to something human and familiar. The conversations had died down, replaced by the rhythmic tapping of computer keys and the occasional weary cough. She could hear the caregivers speaking in low tones, passing files and updating charts.

At the nurses' station, Lindsey approached, drying off her hands on a paper towel as Kate was signing the form for receiving a new patient.

"Did I miss something?" Lindsey said, looking at Harry the way someone would when a person who is supposed to keep a secret let the cat out of the bag by mistake.

Kate tore the top sheet from the printer, scrolled through the form's endless fields of checkboxes, signed the last line, then handed it to Lindsey with a flat "Here you go." Kate looked up at them both, her expression somewhere between annoyance and fatigue.

Harry said nothing.

"Happy Halloween," Lindsey said, collecting the paperwork into her right hand.

An alarm sounded.

Kate snapped her head toward the panel, where a bright red LED blinked next to the room number 103.

"That's Rose's room," Kate said.

Without hesitation, she jogged down the hall, her sneakers squeaking on the polished linoleum.

Harry and Lindsey realized that most of the second shift had already departed for the day, leaving Kate to manage until the third shift nurses arrived, so they stayed and lent a hand.

When Kate reached the door, she flicked on the overhead lights, flooding the room with instant brightness.

The paramedics entered right behind Kate.

Rose was lying flat; eyes shut, the surrounding skin puckered into deep wells. Her color had drained, leaving her cheeks chalky and her lips a strange shade of lavender. If perhaps her lips quivered just moments before, lifelessness had now taken its place.

"Mrs. Windslow?" Kate said, coming to her side.

Rose didn't answer. Her pulse was rapid; her fingers cold.

"Take her to the hospital," Kate said, her voice urgent but steady.

Lindsey and Harry nodded. Seeing the state of the patient, they moved without hesitation to shift Rose from her bed to a transport gurney. Harry started the oxygen, while Lindsey checked her pupils with a small penlight. They wheeled the gurney into the hall.

"I'll fax her chart over," Kate said. She moved John Doe out of the way, allowing the paramedics to hurry toward the ambulance.

Both paramedics moved into action, and within seconds the trio had their cargo loaded into the ambulance and had vanished.

The hallway fell eerily silent.

Kate stood for a moment at the threshold of the now-empty room. Then she turned to look at the gurney that had been waiting outside Rose's door.

With Lindsey and Harry gone, she had to maneuver the gurney into the room by herself, leaving John Doe where Rose had lain only minutes earlier.

She braced her shoulder against the gurney, rolling it over the threshold and setting the brakes with a practiced stomp. She glanced at the man's face, still slack and untroubled, then at his hands, which lay to his side. There was nothing unusual about his appearance except perhaps the paleness of his knuckles and the yellowing of his nails, but the pulse ox monitor on his finger blinked steadily, confirming life.

"Well now, isn't that convenient," Kate muttered.

She felt a low thrill—half fear, half fascination—as she imagined the two patients passing in the hallway, one leaving, one arriving. She thought about what Harry had mentioned earlier about John Doe and passed it off as a Halloween prank. John Doe had been waiting for this room to be empty.

She left the room, closing the door behind her with a soft click.

The nurses' station, humping with duties earlier, now deserted; the only sound was the faint whine of the floor buffer while Jack, the janitor, worked the east wing. Kate sat for a moment, taking a deep breath, and typed a quick incident report on Rose's sudden episode. After finishing, she closed her eyes for a moment of silence. Then, she stood up, collected her clipboard, and began her rounds.

CHAPTER 2

Kate had exited Ethel Wallace's room, leaving behind her fabricated cheerful demeanor to appease Mrs. Wallace, when she collided with a young woman in the hallway. She let out a surprised scream, taken aback by her own jumpiness. Kate dismissed it as Harry the Scaremonger trying to mess with her mind as part of a subtle Halloween trick.

"Oops," the young woman said.

"Visiting hours are over," Kate said. "How did you manage to get in here?"

"My name is Beth Myers," the young woman said. "It's my first day."

"Night," Kate said, correcting her.

"First night," Beth said.

After taking a moment to assess Beth's outfit, Kate instructed, "Follow me." She guided Beth to the nurses' station.

"Why do you smell like smoke? Are you a smoker?" Kate said.

"No," Beth said. "I was by a fire."

"I used to enjoy making s'mores by a campfire," Kate said.

I wasn't referring to a campfire, Beth thought.

"You'll be shadowing Betsy until you become familiar with the rounds," Kate said.

"Who's talking about me?" Betsy said, as she approached the nurses' station clad in a white Halloween-themed scrubs top adorned with black cats, witches' brooms, and hats scattered among the fabric.

Finally, Kate thought, relief had arrived as the nurses scheduled for the next shift began to show up.

A moment later, Tammy arrived, trailing a scent of pumpkin spice. She wore with almost grim devotion, a witch's hat perched askew over her ponytail, and a shirt with two cartoon ghosts wielding syringes above the caption: Boo Boo Crew, I Will Stab You. The ghosts grinned with a manic glee that Tammy herself could never muster. In one hand she clutched a plastic pumpkin pail brimming with fun-sized candy bars; in the other, an already half-emptied coffee thermos.

Beth grinned as Missy came her way, amused by her outfit. Missy wore a costume of her own invention: tan scrubs repurposed as a patient, Cavity Sam on the Operation board game, each felt "body part" stitched on with cartoonish precision—a wishbone, a heart, a lone Adam's apple. The effort was impressive, yet a bit unhinged. In one arm she balanced a lopsided stack of pizza boxes, and under the other, chocolate cupcakes with an edible eyeball in the center of the icing, and a book riding tucked up under her armpit, pinched between her upper arm and bra.

"Who do we have here?" Missy said.

"My name is Beth Myers," Beth said.

"Well, I'm Missy Chenshaw and this is Tammy Bisset and I'm sure you already met Kate Chapman and this is…" Missy said, interrupted by Betsy.

"I'm Betsy Monaghan," Betsy said.

Kate walked off to finish her rounds.

"Oh, and here is the last to arrive as usual," Missy said. "This is Jennifer Givings."

Jennifer approached the gathering, holding a coffee cup in her left hand, a box of thin veggie toasted crackers in her right, and her small purse slung over her right shoulder.

"Hi," Jennifer said. "You must be the new girl."

She took her contact lens case from her right pocket and set it on the counter, placing her bottle of saline solution next to it.

"Yep, that's me," Beth replied.

Jennifer had dressed in a revealing white nurse's costume, complete with white stockings and a vintage nurse's cap adorned with a red cross on her forehead. Skeleton earrings dangled from her earlobes. The petite short dress hugged her figure like a surgical glove, sparking envy in the hearts of other girls. She placed her purse under the counter.

"Beth, you're going to love the graveyard shift. There's absolutely no action," Missy said.

"There's nothing much to do," Tammy said. "Not like the day shift."

"I like watching my nail polish dry," Jennifer said.

"You only need to make it through until the morning shift without dozing off," Betsy remarked. She set down a platter of hotdogs that were crafted to resemble human fingers, with shallow cuts along each knuckle and the casing removed where fingernails ought to be, enhancing the playful illusion.

"Yeah, that's the hardest part," Jennifer said. "That's why I chew gum."

Jennifer was washing her hands in the little sink when she looked over at Beth.

"You want a stick," Jennifer said.

"Maybe later," Beth said.

"I'll have one," Missy said.

"Aww, I just washed my hands to put my contacts in," Jennifer said. "You care to wait until I'm done?"

Missy nodded reluctantly knowing Jennifer would forget by then.

Jennifer took hold of her contact lens case, unscrewed the lids with the dexterity of a surgeon, and set the containers on the counter. She held her eyelid open and, after a moment of concentration, popped the lens onto her eye. She blinked twice, eyes watering.

Beth was standing next to Jennifer when something in Jennifer's lab coat pocket began vibrating.

"Beth, grab my vibrator," Jennifer said, thrusting her right hip pocket toward the new girl.

Beth jumped, caught off guard by the request, and for a split second wondered if this was some kind of hazing ritual. The others erupted in fits of laughter, but their cackling only made it worse.

"You want me to—" Beth started.

Jennifer, balancing her other contact lens on her fingertip, shrugged. "Don't make me beg. I've got saline dripping down my face."

The group was in a riot. Even Betsy, normally locked in her own orbit, laughed so hard she almost dislodged her own glasses.

Beth, cheeks flushed, reached into Jennifer's coat pocket. The vibrator was a slim, sophisticated rectangle—what looked like a high-end cosmetic compact with a pink gingham plaid checkered pattern case. She held it up for inspection. It vibrated again, more urgently this time.

Jennifer did her best imitation of an orgasm face, complete with theatrical breathing.

"Beth, if you only knew where I had that thing before coming to work," she moaned.

Beth fumbled, almost dropping the device.

"No!" the others shouted in unison, half-mocking, half-genuine.

Beth soon realized Jennifer was having fun with her, so she acted in the moment to counter the amusement. She caught it between her palms like it might explode.

"Got you," Beth said, smiled.

She attempted to convince the group, holding on to her poker face, that she was unruffled, but the flush on her cheeks gave away her poker hand. She was embarrassed.

Jennifer took pity, easing up on the theatrics, and instead dripped saline onto her remaining contact.

A momentary silence followed—then Missy, unable to restrain herself, howled with laughter.

Jennifer, not to be outdone, gestured at the compact.

"Open it."

Beth, still uncertain, examined the object.

"But I don't wear makeup," she said.

Beth felt the pause. The group stared as if she'd missed the bus to reality. Betsy's eyebrow arched. Kate just shook her head in disbelief.

"It's my fold-up flip Smartphone," Jennifer said, dropping the act, now being serious.

This thing is a telephone, Beth thought.

Beth managed a sheepish smile. "I knew that. I was just messing with you all."

She flipped open the pink plaid phone and, for the first time, noticed the screen was blank.

"Where's the plug?" Beth said, genuinely perplexed.

"What, the charger?" Jennifer said. "It should have a full charge."

Beth, realizing she was a step behind the times, handed the phone back. "It's not on."

Jennifer laughed, double-tapped the screen, and with a swipe of her thumbprint, unlocked it. The display was already open to a text.

"There you go," Jennifer said, nodding at the phone.

Wow, this is really exciting, Beth thought.

Beth, curious now, read the message out loud. "Working a double. Missing you already."

"He's her man," Missy said.

"Ooh," Tammy said. "Doctor Ben Flanagan."

"Hope he's a gynecologist," Betsy said, not missing a beat.

"Only when we're alone," Jennifer said, a playful glint in her eyes as she lightly stuck her tongue between her front teeth.

Betsy smirked and shook her head while the others laughed.

"Oh my," Missy said, "Did someone just turn up the heat?"

The giggles increased.

Beth's face blushed a little bit more.

"Text back and tell him I'm off tomorrow," Jennifer said. "Say, drinks at Tiffany's tomorrow night."

Beth, eager to prove herself, started typing, but her thumbs moved with the hesitant, searching rhythm of someone who hadn't yet learned the muscle memory of modern texting.

Jennifer craned over her shoulder. "You forgot to hit send," she said. "Here, let me see." She took the phone from Beth and pressed the button herself.

"Oh, sorry," Beth said.

Missy, who fanned the air with the book she'd been hiding under her arm, broke the brief silence.

"I brought this to keep us entertained," Missy said.

She lifted the book for everyone to see. The title read Real Haunts in Real Places.

"This should be interesting," Jennifer said with a skeptical look.

From within the building, the women heard the sky rumble.

"Was that thunder?" Jennifer said. "The weather seemed fine until I arrived at this dreadful place."

"I thought we weren't expecting any rain," Betsy said.

"Look at my hair; it's a mess," Jennifer said.

A sudden beep blared from the ceiling-mounted television. The local weather station came alive on the screen to give those in its listening area a warning of an approaching storm. A red banner crawled across the bottom of the screen, its urgent crawl a siren in text:

TORNADO WATCH IN EFFECT FOR THE FOLLOWING COUNTIES.

Tammy looked up at the television. She saw the weather map displaying the intensity of an incoming storm, marked by a red zone advancing across the state toward them.

"Hey turn up the sound," Tammy said.

The broadcast cut from a commercial for maxi pads, feminine protection, to a studio where a doughy, silver-haired meteorologist stood in front of a digital map. The counties glowed with a lurid, radioactive red. In the lower-left corner, a pixelated tornado icon spun.

"I'm meteorologist Guy Hanson," the man said, "and if you're just now tuning in, this is what we're seeing so far." He gestured with a trembling hand to a crimson blotch swelling eastward across the map; it looked less like a storm and more like a hemorrhage. "This area in the red indicates a severe weather pattern that has the potential of causing tornado activity. The National Weather Service has issued a tornado watch for all of these counties—" he paused to let the list scroll, "—including ours. All these flash icons are lightning, which is occurring every few seconds. Please be advised: if and when you should seek shelter."

Jennifer's fingers drummed against her coffee cup.

The meteorologist's tone shifted, made grave by the weight of civic responsibility: "Those counties scrolling at the bottom of the screen need to listen for sirens in your area. We will be following this storm on our radar. As this storm builds, we will keep you posted. In the event of immediate danger, you will need to stay clear of all windows. Please stay tuned for minute-by-minute updates."

"Wow, that sounds serious," Missy said.

A call came in from Lakeside Memorial Hospital, and Tammy picked up the phone.

"Weather the Storm Nursing Home," she said.

Missy noticed the gravity on Tammy's face and exchanged glances with Betsy. Just then, Kate approached after finishing her rounds, right as Tammy placed the phone back on the cradle.

"What's going on?" Missy said.

"That was Lakeside Hospital," Tammy said.

"And…?" Betsy said.

"Rose is dead," Tammy said. "Everyone in the ambulance perished on the way to the hospital, including Rose."

"That's terrible," Beth said.

"The man said the wind caused the ambulance to lose control and crash into a tree," Tammy said.

The four of them looked to Kate for any sign of compassion, but she showed no remorse.

CHAPTER 3

The nurses started debating who would be the one to call Mr. Windslow. Kate reached over the counter and picked up the landline phone. Missy turned the monitor towards Kate, displaying all of Mrs. Windslow's emergency contact numbers. With a sense of satisfaction, Kate dialed the number to reach Rose's husband.

"Mr. Windslow?" she said.

"Yes," he said.

"This is Weather the Storm Nursing Home," Kate said. "Your wife is dead." She slammed the phone back into its cradle.

"Oh my gosh," Betsy exclaimed. "I can't believe you just said that with no remorse."

"What's the difference? She's dead," Kate said. "There's no point in sugarcoating it; dead is dead.

Besides, he's a man, and men don't have feelings. They're tough macho freaks through and through."

"Here," Jennifer said, tossing a small plastic-wrapped package to her.

Kate looked down at her palm.

"It's a red condom," she said.

"Yeah, you need it more than the rest of us," Jennifer said.

Betsy laughed.

Kate tossed it onto the countertop beside her.

"What happened to Mrs. Windslow?" Tammy said.

"She was unresponsive at first, and since the paramedics were already here with a new patient, I had them take her to the hospital. So, I guess she didn't make it," Kate said.

"Wait, a new patient?" Missy said.

"Yeah, get this, John Doe," Kate said with a grin.

"Where is he now?" Tammy said.

"I placed him in Mrs. Windslow's room," Kate said. "It was the only clean bed available—the orthopedic traction bed with the single overhead bar and traction shelf."

"Hey, whatever works," Betsy said.

Footsteps echoed across the linoleum floor as Jack Jensen, the maintenance man, made his way to the nurse's station. Feeling embarrassed, Kate snatched the condom from the counter and tucked it into the right pocket of her white jacket to keep it hidden from Jack, who was just a few steps away. The lights flickered in response to a thunderclap.

"I've put a pail under the leak in the ladies' restroom," Jack said. "I'll call about the roof tomorrow. No one will come out tonight in this weather."

"I suppose not," Kate said.

"Hey Jack, do you want a slice of pizza? There's no pork on it," Missy offered.

"No, thank you," Jack said as he walked away. Kate rolled her eyes.

"Hey Jack," Kate called out, stopping him before he could get too far.

"Yeah?" Jack said.

"Could you check a light bulb in room 115 for me? It keeps flickering like it's about to go out." The lights above the nurses' station flickered again just before another thunderclap. Jack glanced at the light and then back at Kate, as if blaming the storm for the flickering bulb in room 115.

"It's not the same; this is different," Kate insisted.

"Sure, no problem," Jack said.

"You should know that John Doe is on a ventilator. I've already completed the incident report for Rose," Kate said.

"Go home, Kate," Tammy said. "You look like you've had a rough day. We can handle things from here."

"I'll check John Doe's vitals first, then I'll leave," Kate said.

"Hold on a second," Missy said. She grabbed her phone and handed it to Kate. "Could you take a group photo of the graveyard shift?"

"Sure," Kate said.

Kate snapped a few photos with Missy's phone and then turned to walk away.

"Thanks, Kate," Betsy said. "Make sure you get some rest."

Missy reached for a sucker from the candy bowl and peeled off the wrapper she used for her gum.

"These suckers remind me of the ones you get at the bank," Missy said.

"They're one and the same," Tammy said.

"So, you collect them every time you go until you have enough to give away for trick-or-treating?" Jennifer asked.

"Yep, once a week," Tammy confirmed. "Kids these days always want something for free, so why should I pay for it?"

Missy grimaced.

"So, some of these are a year old?" Missy said.

"Sure," Tammy said, maintained a straight face. "Do you think they expire?"

Missy tossed the sucker into the trash.

"You cheap witch," Jennifer teased.

Tammy grinned.

"Got you," Tammy said. "My trick is your treat."

Betsy threw a paperclip at Tammy while they all shared a laugh.

"Why don't you eat pork? Is it because of some religious belief?" Beth asked Missy.

"I grew up on a farm and had a pet pig named Pinky. One day, while I was at school, my dad cut Pinky's head off, and my mom cooked him for dinner that night," Missy replied. "I promised myself I would never eat pork again."

"That's really sad," Beth said.

"For the pig or for Missy?" Jennifer said.

"Both," Beth said.

"I even wrote a little poem about Pinky," Missy said.

"Pinky, Pinky, where art thou? I expected to see you among the chickens and cows. But while I was at school, Daddy took an axe in hand, and turned Big Pinky into just a little ham. Now Pinky doesn't sleep with me anymore. Pinky is gone forevermore."

"I was just ten years old when I wrote it," Missy said.

"I can feel your sadness," Beth said.

"How about I give you the grand tour?" Jennifer said to Beth.

"Sure," Beth said.

Jennifer led the way, with Beth following, while the others continued to giggle.

As Missy opened the glass door of the refrigerator at the nurse's station to put away a couple of cans of her favorite soda, she noticed the thermostat reading 48 degrees, which was too warm to store insulin. Tammy saw the worried expression on Missy's face.

"What's wrong," Tammy said.

"It's not getting cold," Missy said.

Betsy peered inside and listened for the motor to turn on, but all she heard was silence.

"I think the motor just died," Betsy said.

"What should we do?" Missy said.

"We need to transfer all the insulin to the walk-in refrigerator in the kitchen," Betsy said.

"I'll go grab a cart," Tammy said.

CHAPTER 4

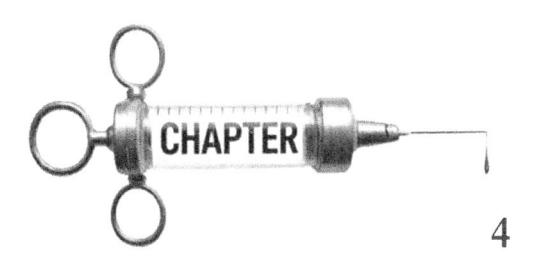

The urine bag that Kate held in her gloved right hand was light, almost insubstantial. She'd expected it to contain at least a few hundred milliliters of discharge—something to affirm John Doe's body was carrying out its normal function. Instead, the thin, clear tube that snaked from the base of John Doe's gown ended in a dry, crinkled pouch. She concluded the paramedics must have handled the matter en route.

"Good for them," she said to herself as she stripped off her gloves. She flexed her fingers, then set herself to the next task—assessing his vitals.

Kate approached John Doe's right side and lifted his arm; the limb offered no resistance. She wondered, as she wrapped the cuff around his upper arm, when the last time was that this body had moved of its own will. After placing the stethoscope over the brachial artery, she started inflating the cuff. At 160 millimeters, she started the slow bleed-off of pressure while listening for a pulse. Silence. As she deflated the cuff, she lifted the manometer to eye level, waiting for the first sound through the stethoscope to indicate the systolic pressure. While watching the gauge, she anticipated the sound would fade, giving her the diastolic reading, but her attention got diverted. In her line of vision beyond the manometer, she noticed a bulge just below the center of John Doe's hips. The cuff had deflated, and she missed the second reading.

"Well, that's something I haven't seen in a while," Kate said, gazing beyond the manometer at the rocket raised for a vertical ascent beneath John Doe's gown. It appeared ready to launch. Kate thought for a moment of bread dough rising in the oven.

Her eyes flicked to his face—no change there. Lights out, nobody home. She lifted the sheet for a closer look. She mouthed the words "oh my gosh," though she never vocalized them.

"Well, hello there?" Kate said to John Doe's soldier standing at attention. "So that's why you're not producing any urine; your hose came out. I'll need to clean you up."

From the bathroom, Kate retrieved the rose-hued seven-quart plastic wash basin, a few towels, and some soap. As she prepared to give John Doe his bed bath, an unsettling thought crossed her mind.

Her thoughts drifted back to when Jennifer had tossed a condom at her, scolding her for her behavior. She fished the condom out of her jacket pocket, staring at it as if it were a new discovery. Initially, she had intended to dispose of it, but it had slipped her mind until now. Perhaps this wasn't exactly what her friend had envisioned, but what did it matter? No one would check on him for at least an hour since she had informed the others that she would see to him before heading home, she reasoned. Even if someone walked in, she could always claim that the hose came out, and she was trying to fit it back in. On second thought, that might not be the best way to phrase it. People have done stranger things than this, haven't they? I'll just tidy things up afterward, and no one will be the wiser, she reassured herself.

With her teeth, she tore a small opening in the plastic wrapper, allowing her fingers to take hold. Out came the red condom, and she giggled as she shook it, watching it jiggle. Turning to John Doe, she felt around blindly under the sheet, navigating by touch until she located what she was searching for, and then with one-handed motion, pinched the tip of the condom and unrolled it onto his erect member. She drew back her hands and, with sudden urgency, reached beneath her skirt for her own undergarment. She hooked her thumbs into the elastic of her white cotton panties, yanked them down her thighs, and let them puddle around her ankles. She alternated her feet in a clumsy dance until she was free of the tangled restraint. Then she bunched the discarded underwear into her fist and stuffed it deep into the right-hand pocket of her jacket. The sensation of cool air against her bare skin only heightened her sense of recklessness.

She climbed onto the mattress with the cautious determination of a gymnast preparing for the beam. She planted her knees on either side of his hips and steadied herself with her left hand on the bed's overhead trapeze bar, a sturdy center rail that ran from the headboard to the footboard. The bar was there for patient mobility, but now it was her anchor, the one element of stability in an ocean of uncertainty. She turned herself so she was facing the far wall, her back to his chest, and with her right hand reached beneath her skirt, feeling for the rigid, latex-wrapped shape she had prepared. Leaning forward just a little, while breathing through her nose, long and slow, until she located the tip and maneuvered it into position with the kind of gentle care she reserved for the most delicate of IV insertions. At that instant, she felt a powerful tremor in her thighs, a shivering prelude she could not suppress. She steadied herself with a second hand to the trapeze bar, closed her eyes and took her time lowered herself onto him with a controlled gentleness, letting her weight settle only as far as she dared, easing back into a seated position with her back with the slightest arched. She rocked her hips, taking a slow pace at first, testing the boundaries of her own arousal and his passive resistance. There was a bizarre intimacy to the act, made even more surreal by the absence of a response from the body below her. The only sounds were the soft rasp of her breath and the faint creak of the bed frame as she moved in earnest, staccato at first, then in a slow, deliberate rhythm. She let go of the bar, freeing her hands, and caught sight of her own reflection in the mirror. The image startled her—straddling the inert figure, red hair loose and wild, cheeks flushed beyond the limits of shame or decency. She looked, for the first time in years, alive. Her left hand drifted to the hollow at the base of her neck. The cold sensation of bare metal on her skin reminded her of the thin gold band of her wedding ring. She hesitated for a moment, then slid the ring from her finger and tucked it into her pocket beside the panties.

She continued to shift her hips as if riding a horse at a trot. Her breathing became deeper; her eyelids fluttered open and closed as if awakening from a slumber. Her lips softened, then her jaw dropped as she took a quick breath through her open mouth, exhaling in moderation through a small opening formed by her puckered lips as if preparing to kiss someone. She took her time to relish the sensation. When her eyes opened again, she saw her reflection in the mirror biting her bottom lip. The sensation of his presence inside her was at once eerie and electric, thrilling her to the core. He was hard enough to cut diamonds, more so than any conscious man she'd ever known, and the reality that this resulted from some neural misfire or chemical imbalance only amplified the forbidden pleasure of it. She began to move faster, grinding her hips in a figure-eight, toes digging into the mattress for leverage. Her breathing grew ragged, her mouth opened in a silent gasp, and the reflection in the glass became a blur of motion and color. Gone was the competent nurse; in her place was a creature of pure appetite. She thought for a moment of her husband—his face, his voice, the way he used to touch her before the long silences and the icy standoffs. She thought about how out-of-the-norm this was for her, and how she would explain to her husband if she lost her job over it—but the thought evaporated as fast as it formed. She surprised herself at how little she cared about the consequences.

Mother always told me whenever opportunity arises, don't hesitate, she thought. I'm pretty sure this wasn't what she had in mind when she was giving me that advice.

The thought made her laugh, a guttural, involuntary sound that startled her even as it escaped. Kate quickened her pace, applying more pressure and delivering more forceful rubs with each escalating moan. If this guy was going to meet his end, she was determined to give him the time of his life beforehand. The intensity of her moans grew louder. She wasn't concerned about the thin walls, as most residents struggled with hearing loss. As her climax built, she clenched her fists tight enough to make her knuckles turn white, and the entire bed shuddered beneath her in a crescendo of sound. She bit down on her lower lip so hard she tasted blood, but she did not stop, did not slow down, did not even try to stifle the moans that rose unbidden from her chest. The sounds echoed off the tile and ceiling, merging with the hum of the ventilators and the distant murmur of the nurses' station. For a moment, she was certain the whole world could hear her, that her shame and triumph had become a public spectacle, but even that thought only made her want more. The bed creaked, a metallic, arrhythmic percussion that kept time with her breathing. Kate braced herself by placing her hands on John Doe's thighs, resembling a gymnast balancing on parallel bars, a thought that felt strange, especially since the only instance of women competing on such apparatus was during the 1936 Olympics in Berlin, and they have reserved it only for men ever since. She couldn't quite grasp why that thought had invaded her mind at this moment. To divert her thoughts, she looked down at his legs, which were draped in a sheet that resembled two Indian burial mounds protruding from the earth, similar to the Serpent Mound in Ohio. She couldn't help but see the tan line on her ring finger where her wedding band had rested just minutes earlier. She was commandeering John Doe, using his body, like in the Bible story of Lot and his two daughters, who raped their own father so as not to be childless. This act represented Kate's assertion of power and control in a male-dominated world, fueling her desire to take him deeper. However, as she pushed further, the more her mind fractured. Out of nowhere, the thought of Sigmund Freud's theory that all girls suffer from penis envy made it more difficult for her to concentrate. She tried to chase the intrusive thoughts away, but they ricocheted around her skull like steel ball bearings. She felt like a thief, a trespasser, a desecrator, and yet here she was, legs spread wide, straddling the literal boundary between dignity and disgrace. There was no love in it, no romance, only the cold harsh certainty of action and reaction, a Newtonian inevitability that made her feel at once omnipotent and utterly doomed. There was nothing mutual in the deed. Had he consented, she would've refused. This would be her own secret, her own little act of rebellion against nature's cruel punishment towards her husband. She saw herself at that moment as a Valkyrie, riding through the carnage of her own failed life, harvesting whatever pleasure she could from the battlefield of her disappointments. A man in a coma presented the ideal situation; there were no annoying phone calls, no need to sneak around, no breakups, no obligations, and no harassment.

While some women have a passion for collecting dolls, I find myself drawn to an action-figure; she thought with amusement.

She was aware of every internal sensation, every inch of friction, shuddering pull inside her. She dug her nails into his thigh; the skin was unyielding. He did not flinch, did not react, and that made her want it more. Every thrust was a small act of vengeance against nature. She pressed herself down harder, grinding her sensitive bump against the base of his shaft. She felt the climax building, relentless and hot. She could feel the drumbeat of her own pulse in her thighs, her muscles trembling.

She was close, so close, and she did not want to stop, not for anything, not even for the gnawing sense that something was very wrong. She ignored the feeling of fullness inside her that seemed to intensify with every movement, chalking it up to the novelty, the perversity, the sheer insanity of what she was doing.

But then, in the space between two heartbeats, everything changed.

Just as she was about to unleash all her frustrations, depression, anger, and the countless irritating disappointments of life in one overwhelming gushing moment, she stopped, her eyes wide in shock. John Doe was growing inside her, and not in a pleasant way. She felt him moving inside her—an expansion, a swelling, as if muscle and tissue and bone had regenerated, to pulse with a life of their own. It was not the spasmodic twitch of involuntary reflex; it was a deliberate, alien stretching, an inhuman growth reaching parts of her insides not possible with a man's anatomy. She jerked her hips back in alarm, but found herself unable to dislodge him. Together they fused as one, locked like two canines mating, the knot inside her growing tighter, more insistent. Panic surged through her, obliterating the last remnants of pleasure. She whipped her head around to look at his face. Still blank, still slack-jawed, still utterly unresponsive. She became aware with mounting horror that the pain was not just internal, but radiating outward, into her pelvis, her hips, her lower spine. It was as if something inside her was burrowing, tunneling, seeking fresh territory. The sensation was overwhelming, a volcanic pressure that threatened to tear her apart. What had felt like bliss just moments ago had shifted to torment. The sensation was no longer one of being filled, but of being consumed. Turning back to the mirror, she caught sight of her own reflection—painful, worried, with two red lights glowing from John Doe's eyes. She looked back at him, and the lights had vanished. When she turned her gaze forward again, she noticed her favorite pair—Victoria's Secret, white with pink floral and a lace waistband, bikini cut panties dangling from the adjustment knob on the overhead trapeze, right in front of her like some bizarre, white guillotine. Disgust washed over her as her eyes locked on the gusset, which was no longer pristine, but streaked with a viscous, cream-colored discharge—Boutique Beige. Confused and panicked, her instinct was to reach into her jacket pocket, doubting the obvious, but the only thing she retrieved was her wedding ring, which she held between her thumb and index finger. An unexpected, intense throb of pain, reminiscent of childbirth, surged within her, leaving her gasping. She dropped the ring and grabbed the sheet as if it could alleviate the suffering. The ring fell with an audible ping onto the linoleum, making a sound similar to a small bell. She felt as though she were being tortured. There was a fleeting image in her mind—a bell tolling, marking the hour of her own undoing. The pain did not abate. If anything, it intensified, radiating outward from her core. She clutched at the bedsheet, tearing at it with her nails, the white fabric offering no comfort, no purchase. She wanted to scream, but the noise that came out was nothing more than a strangled whimper, almost inaudible above the mechanical whir of the ventilator and the distant, ominous rumble of thunder from above. The ventilator was pumping faster and faster. She could hear the faint strains of a T.V. in the next room—a newscaster reciting storm warnings but the storm outside was nothing compared to the tornado tearing through her body. She glanced down in shock, horrified, her eyes widening as she noticed her stomach bulging outward and then contracting in uneven, twitching bursts, as though she had ingested a brush handle. The sheet was now soaked with sweat, his hospital gown clinging to her back. She tried again to pull away, but her hips were locked in place, as if two invisible hands had clamped down and would not release her. She was not a religious woman, but she would have done anything for deliverance in that moment.

I'd be fortunate if someone could hear me over the roar of the thunder, she thought. Things could go so wrong so fast in so many ways.

The light fixture above the bed flickered a strobe rhythm.

This situation couldn't continue like this. She might lose consciousness. With her arms pinned against her sides, fatigue settled into her limbs. What followed was beyond what she could've predicted. An unseen force pulled her head toward her hanging panties. A sudden, sharp jerk wrenched her head forward so fast her vision swam. She tried to resist, to brace her neck, but her own body betrayed her. She was being pulled, not by hands, but by a force that was neither gravity nor physics nor even biology. It was as if an enormous, invisible magnet existed somewhere in the room, tugging at her iron skull. She wanted to scream, but her jaw wouldn't open. Her teeth clenched so hard she could feel the enamel crack in protest. Drool filled her mouth and ran down her chin, pooling in the hollow of her collarbone. She would have bitten through her own tongue if she had thought it would bring relief, or at least some control, but she was on rails now, on a ride she could neither pause nor derail. Her body was the coaster, and she was just a passenger, buckled in for the duration. Her arms, still pinned to her sides, offered no resistance as the underwear moved, inching forward with predatory patience. The opening stretched wide, the elastic picot waistband flexing in slow motion, and she realized with perfect clarity what was about to happen. Her body, despite its mutiny, registered the full horror of it. The discharge was cold and clammy like fresh sweat, and it smelled of a hint of floral detergent mixed with her own scent, a combination that made her stomach churn. The panties slipped over her forehead with a practiced ease, catching at her ears before snapping down to her neck. She thrashed her head, but it made no difference. The elastic scalloped lace dug deeper, compressing her windpipe, making each breath a struggle between agony and panic. The ventilator was pumping even faster. If there was ever a time to scream, now was that moment, she thought. A supernatural force was probing her thoughts. She attempted to scream, but the gusset pressed firm against her throat, choking her. Every time she tried to suck in air, the gusset sealed tighter, flattening her trachea. She could hear her own heartbeat now, pounding in her ears, drowning out even the distant sounds of the nursing home. It was a countdown, a drumroll leading up to the final act. She tried one last time to reach the call button. Her hand inched toward it, centimeters at a time, but her fingers wouldn't close, wouldn't grip. The button's cord swung just out of range. She might as well have been shackled to the bed. Fatigue rolled through her, heavy and slick, and she realized she was losing consciousness. The darkness came in waves, each one longer and more complete than the last, but just before she fully blacked out, the world snapped back into focus, sharper and more merciless than before. She tried to scream again, but the panties worked as a gag, compressing her esophagus so nothing but a thin whistle escaped. Her own breath was the only sound. The pain was so intense that it numbed her brain, fuzzing out the edges of her consciousness. She wanted to vomit, but her throat had constricted to prevent it. She could taste bile rising, mingling with the coppery blood and the taste of cotton. A prickling sensation coursed down her legs, and her thighs felt numb, like when one sits too long on the toilet, restricting blood flow. Her heart pounded with anxiety.

She thought of her mother, of the words she'd once used to comfort Kate after a childhood fall. "Sometimes the pain gets worse before it gets better," she'd said, dabbing at Kate's scraped knees with a cotton ball soaked in peroxide. "But you're strong enough, I know you are." The memory brought no comfort now, only a sense of vast cosmic irony. She hoped her mother would never find out how she had died. She hoped no one would.

Her chance of escape had slipped away. She couldn't shake the thought that she was being hanged by the very underwear she had worn throughout the day. Breathing turned into a challenge. She wished someone would check on John Doe. The humiliation no longer mattered; she could relocate and find another job. Discovery while alive held the greatest value. She never envisioned her life would end like this. Images of her bitter responses during a heartless conversation with Jed flashed through her thoughts.

Wow, you do have a lot on your mind. Should I just leave you to wallow in your sorrows? Perhaps I could drop off a box of tissues to you while I attend to more important things. I mean I would say you need to forget the past and get on with your life but you don't have a life, do you? All you have to hold on to is your history.

Jed had only wanted compassion, and now she regretted how she had responded. She wished she could take back her words.

As the light faded, she realized she would reach the other side before Jed, wherever that may be. It was one competition she would willingly accept defeat in. Why hadn't she left when she had the chance? Tears flowed down her cheeks as she contemplated the heartache she would leave for her husband. The red eyes watched in the mirror faded into darkness.

The ventilator resumed its normal speed.

In that moment, Kate was dead. Her final thought she carried into the next realm echoed the same word Jed had warned her about: Karma.

CHAPTER 5

After exploring the chapel, Jennifer guided Beth through a door that opened into a spacious room, which housed several filled wooden bookcases, a worn conference table, and an antique upright piano.

"This is our charming little library," Jennifer said, beaming.

"Where do all these books come from?" Beth said, pointing at the bookcases filled bookcases.

"Most of them were donated," Jennifer said.

"By whom?" Beth said.

"Mainly by the families of patients," Jennifer said. "When someone passes away, the family often just wants to get rid of everything."

Beth's attention led her to the framed photographs on the wall across the room. They were old black-and-white images of teachers and students from the Weather the Storm girls' school for the blind and deaf. The children appeared to be between five and twelve years old. The images were formal, taken outside in what must have been this same building's grounds half a century ago, the backdrop recognizable even through the distortion of time and the blizzard of gray static that passed for grass and sky in the old prints. Rows of children, all girls, some in thick glasses, others staring into the lens with an unsettling, unblinking intensity. Teachers behind them, their faces pale above the dark blots of their suits and dresses.

"I feel sorry for them," Beth said, gazing at the photographs. She realized her voice was softer than she had intended, almost muffled by the air.

"The deceased or the families?" Jennifer said.

For a moment, Beth allowed herself to drift in the in-between realm of the living and the dead; while reflecting on her own past through the perspective of those young girls, the permanence of their absence weighed heavy on Beth's heart as she gazes at the photographs, the empty spaces where they used to be a constant reminder of their loss. She can almost see their ghosts lingering in the room, their presence forever etched into her memories. When she looked away from the pictures, she noticed Jennifer was waiting for her response.

"For both," Beth said.

Now intrigued, Jennifer wanted to know what had caught Beth's attention.

Jennifer leaned in beside her, her hair brushing Beth's shoulder.

"That's interesting," Jennifer said.

Beth glanced at her sidelong.

"What do you mean?" Beth said.

"I've never seen these here before," Jennifer said. "I wonder who put them up."

"You've never noticed them until now?" Beth said.

"No," Jennifer said, shaking her head. She leaned in for a closer look. "Hey."

"What's wrong," Beth said, her tone revealing that she was concealing something.

Jennifer didn't pick up on Beth's all-of-a-sudden nervousness; if she did, she didn't let on.

"He's kind of cute," Jennifer said, gesturing toward a man standing near a flagpole.

"That's Jed," Beth said, immediately regretting that she had mentioned his name.

Jennifer laughed.

"We have a resident named Jed," Jennifer said, her gaze still fixed on the photograph. Her laughter implied that she thought Beth was joking by connecting the man in the photograph to a name she recognized, but Beth's expression was sincere. When Jennifer turned to face Beth, she noticed Beth deep in thought as if she were solving a crossword puzzle. "Jed Meyers."

"Interesting," Beth said.

"Wait a second. You two share the same last name," Jennifer said, as if she'd just realized the similarities.

"What a coincidence," Beth said.

"Do you know him?" Jennifer said.

"No relation that I'm aware of," Beth said.

Jennifer turned back to face the photograph.

"This photo looks like it was taken over fifty years ago," Jennifer said.

"Fifty-nine years, actually," Beth said.

"How do you know that?" Jennifer said.

"It's labeled as such," Beth said.

"Where?" Jennifer said.

"On the back," Beth said.

Jennifer picked up one of the picture frame from the wall and examined the back.

This photo was taken on October 17th, 1966, just thirteen days prior to the fire.

Jennifer stared at Beth as if she were from another planet.

"But you've never checked the back of these photos, have you?" Jennifer said.

"I must've come across information while doing research at the public library," Beth said.

"Why would you go to the library when you can find everything you need by browsing the internet on your phone?" Jennifer said.

Browsing the internet, Beth thought. What is she even talking about?

"I must've misplaced it," Beth said.

"You can't be serious. I mean, you can misplace your car keys or even your kids, but no one loses their phone," Jennifer said.

"Well, I'd hate to think someone might've stolen it," Beth said.

"To me, that would rank up there with committing a mortal sin," Jennifer said.

"For years people managed perfectly fine without a handheld phone," Beth said. "Besides, I prefer the library. I love the atmosphere."

Jennifer returned the picture to its spot on the wall.

"Come on, let's check out the kitchen," Jennifer said, walking away.

Beth took another glance at the photograph before following Jennifer.

One teacher in the photo bore a striking resemblance to Beth. The similarity was remarkably consistent.

CHAPTER 6

Jennifer paused at the nurses' station while Beth stepped into the restroom.

"Where's Beth?" Betsy said, glancing up from her phone.

Jennifer tucked a loose strand of hair behind her ear.

"She went to the ladies' room," Jennifer said. "You having any luck?" Jennifer was referring to Betsy's phone.

"Nope, not even a single bar," Betsy said. "This thing is useless tonight."

"I can't get a signal either," Jennifer said, shifting her weight from one foot to the other. "I texted Ben about Rose, but I'm not sure it went through."

"Is there something else bothering you besides Rose?" Betsy said.

"It's Beth," Jennifer said.

"What about Beth?" Tammy said.

"She's claimed to have misplaced her phone," Jennifer said.

"She doesn't have a phone?" Tammy said, surprised.

"No, and I sense she's never had one," Jennifer said.

"That's not too unusual," Betsy said, "according to statistics, about one-third of the world's population has never made a phone call."

"How would you know that?" Tammy said.

"I was at the license bureau waiting to renew my license when I saw that trivia question on the monitor," Betsy said.

"And that drew your attention?" Tammy said.

"Do you know how boring it is at the license bureau?" Betsy said.

"Yes, it's dreadful," Jennifer said.

"I'd rather change a diaper," Tammy said.

"It's just… I feel so bad for Beth," Jennifer said. "She probably isn't able to afford one and is too embarrassed to admit it."

Tammy smirked. "Want a finger?" She gestured toward the platter. Hotdogs laid in rows prepared to resemble ghoulish, stubby digits—some with well-trimmed almond slivers as nails, while others had ketchup pooled at the knuckle, giving the impression of having just been severed.

Jennifer wrinkled her nose.

"My gosh, it's hot in here," Jennifer said. "My panties are getting wet for all the wrong reasons."

Tammy and Betsy laughed.

Jennifer gestured at the battered plastic desk fan, which was unplugged in favor of a string of orange lights. "Missy, would you mind plugging in that fan?"

Before Jennifer had walked up, Missy had popped a few Zotz candies into her mouth, letting her saliva mix with the tartaric and malic acids and the bicarbonate that caused a fizz and made her eyes water.

She wiped her hands on her scrubs and reached for the plug. Pressure was building in her mouth, making it hard to suppress the fizz from escaping her nostrils, and with cheeks puffed, she struggled to keep a straight face. When she connected the male end to the female outlet, she convulsed, foam fizzing out of her mouth in a grotesque parody of a seizure. Her antics startled

Betsy for a moment, especially when Missy began shaking with uncontrollable jerky movements.

Concern spread across everyone's faces as they watched her. Seizing the moment, Missy shrieked with laughter, the sound high and unhinged. The "foam" was just the aftermath of her candy, and her jerky movements resolved into a kind of twitchy dance. She said, "Trick or treat" before doubling over in glee.

Tammy, voice sharp and a little too loud, barked, "Missy, you nearly gave me a coronary." But she was smiling, too, her hand pressed to her chest in a gesture of mock-relief. Betsy, ever the mom, handed Missy a handful of tissues to mop up the slobber.

Jennifer rolled her eyes, a half-smirk on her lips.

Missy grinned; bits of tissue stuck to her lips. She tugged on a string tethered to a floating balloon featuring a jack-o'-lantern. She bit into the latex, making a slit just large enough to siphon off a lungful of helium.

"I'm going to grab some coffee before I check on Beth," Jennifer said. "Does anyone want anything?"

"I want candy," Missy said. Her words came out an octave too high, a chipmunk-like pitch from the helium.

Jennifer walked away smiling, leaving the rest of the other women laughing like teenagers. The women's laughter followed her down the hall, echoing in the linoleum corridor. For a moment, she let the sound guide her—an antidote to the dark, the silence.

The lights in the hallway flickered, then steadied. Someone had stuck a construction-paper skeleton on the door of the supply closet. Its arms, raised in surrender; its grin was too wide, too eager. In twelve minutes, Halloween would be officially over. For Jennifer, that couldn't come soon enough. She couldn't wait for things to return to normal.

CHAPTER 7

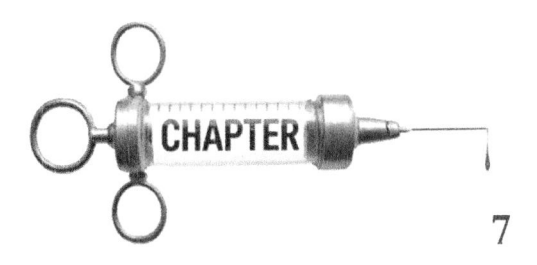

Beth entered the women's restroom, sidestepping a bucket Jack had placed on the floor to catch the leak from the ceiling. The room had an unpleasant scent—humid, metallic, fungal. A quick glance revealed the bucket was about ten percent full. The familiar fluorescent hum vibrated overhead and cast a jaundiced sheen across the off-pink tiles.

Her gaze tracked from the bucket to the ceiling, contemplating the extent of the damage. She weighed the likelihood of being caught in the middle of taking care of business and the ceiling collapsing on her, leading to the bucket of water tipping over, spilling onto the floor around her shoes, while electrical shorts in the ceiling causing a blue tongue of electricity arc straight down to the metal stall door, the flush handle, to her body and electrocuting her while sitting on the toilet.

She had read about this somewhere, maybe in a tabloid at a checkout line: woman electrocuted in her own bathroom, the tragic, undignified death. A nurse somewhere in the Midwest found fused to a plastic toilet seat. For just a moment, Beth pictured the newspaper headline—LOCAL RN DIES IN FREAK RESTROOM INCIDENT—and shuddered at the thought of dying or being knocked unconscious, only for Jack to discover her when he came in to empty the bucket, seeing her there with her white panties around her ankles and a large sanitary napkin clinging to her gusset, exposed and vulnerable.

After a moment's thought, she decided the situation was safe enough for her to chance.

Just before entering the stall, Beth grabbed a free sanitary napkin from the wall dispenser. She lifted her skirt and pulled down her panties; settling her buttocks on the cold toilet seat where she began to pee.

The constant dripping into the bucket was distracting.

Beth reached for her blood-stained pad, and the distinct sound of it peeling away like a sticky nametag being ripped from a shirt resonated within the proximity of the walls. Just then, a loud thunderclap echoed above the ceiling, and the lights went out.

CHAPTER 8

In 1950, Alfred Opus offered his services for killing in the Korean War. As a soldier, he learned to catch sleep in combat situations wherever and whenever possible, often using his backpack as a pillow. Like many of his fellow servicemen, he suffered from hearing loss because of the constant exposure to explosions and gunfire. He had outlasted his squad, his wife, and most of his hearing. Now, at ninety-two, Alfred sleeps well in room 115, while Jack, the maintenance man, stands on a ladder inspecting a flickering fluorescent light without causing a stir. The ladder creaked under his weight as he peered up at the light.

When Alfred's snores grew louder, Jack glanced down at him, shook his head, and continued his work, amazed that Alfred could sleep through the racket. Missy had assured him it would be fine, and now Jack convinced himself that Alfred could sleep through anything, even a tornado if the storm outside intensified. The fluorescent tube blinked on and off like a light in a haunted Halloween attraction. When Jack twisted the tube, the room plunged into total darkness and fell silent, with Alfred's snoring vanishing. However, when Jack twisted the tube again, the light illuminated the room, and Alfred's snores returned even louder.

"Now that's peculiar," Jack thought.

He twisted the glass tube over and over, achieving the same effect; the room fell silent, and Alfred's snores ceased. But then, Jack noticed two glowing red eyes appear in his peripheral vision, just at the level of the six-foot ladder's second rung from the top. Jack turned toward the glowing eyes, but they vanished, only to reappear on his right, as if someone or something had moved behind him. He attempted to turn the tube to restore the light but lost his grip when the ladder jolted, as if kicked. The sound of breaking glass confirmed that the fluorescent light had fallen and shattered on the linoleum floor.

"Who's there?" Jack called out. "Missy, if that's you, this isn't funny. There's broken glass on the floor, and someone could get hurt."

His courage faltering, Jack felt the ladder shake again, and then again, and a fourth time. With each jolt, the glowing red eyes vanished from one spot and reappeared in another around the room. Jack jumped off the ladder and grabbed his cell phone, intending to use its flashlight to unravel the mystery. When he turned on the lights, Alfred's snores resumed. Jack's gaze swept the floor, but no broken glass was visible—the fluorescent tube remained secured in the fixture.

A chattering noise emerged from the side table next to Alfred's bed. It was Alfred's false teeth. He bent closer, compelled by a curiosity that eclipsed his fear. Initially, Jack thought they were vibrating from some ground tremors. The sight was almost humorous, reminding him of wind-up novelty chattering teeth from a magic store people purchase as gag gifts. As he approached, he could discern words.

"Trick or treat," the dentures said.

Jack's scalp prickled. He backed away, tripping over the legs of the walker.

The teeth repeated their phrase, faster now, their clatter rising in tempo and pitch as if competing with Alfred's snores for dominance.

Jack eased back onto the windowsill, leaving him unable to retreat any further.

"Trick or treat," the voice insisted, each repetition louder, the teeth clacking with a manic, almost joyous rhythm.

Jack could not look away. He could not move. He stared at the quivering teeth, which appeared to be shivering, while Alfred continued to snore with his hands folded over his chest as if rehearsing for the casket.

CHAPTER 9

Jennifer entered the canteen in the nurses' lounge to grab a cup of coffee. She stared at the options stamped in shiny laminate: Fresh Brew Coffee, Decaf Coffee, Sugar and Cream, Hot Chocolate, Gourmet Tea Drinks. After she made her choice, a disposable paper cup from within the machine dropped and began filling with a hiss, then gurgled. She bent to inspect the flow. It didn't smell like coffee. The fluid sluiced into the cup in thick, spurting jets, splashing against the sides and pooling at the bottom. When it climbed to the brim, Jennifer reached for it. The overflow cascaded down her fingers in a syrupy tide of deep crimson. Blood clots folded over the edge of the cup like sticky rubber bands. She recoiled; mimicking being scalded. The liquid was warm, almost hot. She couldn't help but stare at the blood dripping from her right hand as if in disbelief. She looked at the splatter on the countertop that ran, a slow ooze that crept toward the edge. The smell hit her then—rusty, primal, the scent of old pennies and fresh wounds. She opened her mouth to call for help, but her vocal cords constricted, failing her, and she found herself silent, the only sound the low hum of the vending machines and the faint, wet patter of droplets striking linoleum. She looked back at the beverage machine, her hand trembling. The light panel above the selection buttons had changed. Where it had read Fresh Brew Coffee before, the lettering now shimmered with a faint red glow and resolved into Fresh Menstrual Blood. The words were clear, unambiguous, seared onto her retinas in the same garish font as always but now bristling with a horror that felt at once ancient and new. Jennifer staggered backward, her breath catching in her chest. She wiped her palm on a napkin, but the stain only smeared, growing more vivid the harder she tried to erase it. Desperate for an anchor in reality, her eyes darted to the candy and chip vending machines where she had purchased her gum earlier, but they had transformed too. The spirals that had once cradled chips and candy bars now held rows of vials labeled Cyanide, Poison, AZT, Venom, Remdezivear, and Toxins. She grimaced at the machine's monstrous inventory.

The mid-section displayed surgical instruments used in lobotomies, including scalpels—one with a rusted blade, another with a tip bent, the long-handled leucotome, the slender wire loop of a Gigli saw, and the Ice Pick. The ice pick's shaft looked stained at the tip with something brown and crusted, the handle worn smooth in places where a thumb might grip it for leverage.

On the upper tier, the coiled wires now supported glistening, wet organs: kidneys, brains, and hearts. They weren't models, weren't props; these were the genuine body parts, leaking a thin, mucous film that pooled at the trough below. Her eyes focused on a heart, fresh, vibrant and pulsating, with the left ventricle contracting and relaxing, propelling thick, crimson arterial blood from the severed end of the aorta in a rhythm. The arterial spray splattered across the glass, forming branching patterns that cascaded down the inner panel, transforming the vending machine compartment into a gruesome spectacle. To further complicate the mystery, there was no blood source supplying the heart. The spiral took its time to rotate, making a faint clicking noise as it worked the heart forward, closer and closer to the edge. Her lips twitched. She wanted to turn away, but her body remained rooted, locked in the moment, paralyzed. The heart finally broke free and tumbled from its bracket, hitting the glass window with a splatter, leaving a bloody smear as it fell into the retrieval compartment with a wet slap. The heart was still beating. The collection trough below the machine overflowed, and red fluid seeped from the seams, wetting the linoleum. Jennifer's eyes watered, her vision blurring, but she couldn't blink, couldn't look away. Her stomach rebelled. The world around her swayed, and she clutched at the countertop to steady herself. Gasping for air, she covered her mouth, trying to suppress the urge to vomit, but the overwhelming stench was too much. She made a break for the wastebasket by the door, her dignity abandoned, and managed to open the lid before she retched. She hadn't given up all she had, but what little she gave made her eyes water.

When she could stand again, Jennifer wiped her lips with the back of a trembling hand and spat into the bin. The taste was still there, metallic and unyielding. She pressed herself against the wall, inching sideways towards the exit, as if afraid to turn her back on the machines. She slowly backed away, but once she was clear of the threshold, she dashed to make a difference in distance in the shortest amount of time between herself and the horrifying scene.

In the windowless restroom, the darkness rendered Beth's vision useless. It was so dark she had to rely on her sense of touch to complete her task. She heard the door creak open.

"Hello," Beth said.

There was no response.

"I'm almost finished," Beth said. "Could you please give me a moment?"

Again, silence filled the air.

Beth felt for the gap in the door, trying to peek outside.

What she saw sent chills down her spine—two red glowing lights, resembling eyes, fixating on her. Those eyes moved closer to her stall.

Beth let out a scream, and the sound reverberated down the hallway.

At the nurses' station, Betsy and Tammy paused mid-conversation.

Betsy rushed to assist Beth.

Jennifer, who was horror-struck in a hurry-scurry; not watching where she was going; frequently glancing back as though something might be pursuing her from behind; collided with Betsy, who was coming down the corridor.

"Whoa, slow down," Betsy said. "Are you alright?"

"Yeah, I was just…," Jennifer said, searching for an excuse that didn't involve what she had just witnessed.

"Did you hear Beth screaming?" Betsy said.

"Yeah, that's where I was going," Jennifer lied. She hadn't heard Beth. She looked down at her trembling hands, expecting to see blood on them but found them to appear normal instead.

Betsy observed Jennifer's unsteady hands and the worried expression on her face.

They both started making their way to the restroom where Beth was.

"Oh my gosh, Jennifer, you look like you just saw a ghost," Betsy said. "Actually, you look as pale as one."

"I'm fine. I just hope Beth is okay," Jennifer said.

"Right," Betsy said.

When Betsy opened the woman's restroom, the lights were on and everything appeared normal, except.

"My gosh, Beth, what did you have for dinner?" Betsy said.

The queasy feeling in Jennifer's stomach resurfaced, but she kept it together. She turned on the ceiling fan to help dissipate the foul odor.

"Beth, are you okay?" Jennifer said.

"I'm fine," Beth said.

"We heard you scream," Betsy said.

Beth emerged from the stall.

"The lights went out, and it felt like a spider or something fell from the ceiling into my hair," Beth lied.

"It was probably just water from the ceiling," Jennifer said.

Betsy glanced down at the bucket.

"Did you drop your used pad in the bucket thinking it was the trash?" To Betsy, blood was spilling over the rim of the bucket. She looked up at the ceiling, where a clear wet spot was visible. "You need to clean this up before the janitor sees it," Betsy said. "If he reports this to Dr. Limpbeck... Let's just say I can do without a lecture on the proper disposal of sanitary napkins."

Beth exchanged a confused look with Jennifer, who seemed equally baffled by Betsy's comments. To Beth, the bucket contained about ten percent clear water, and the ceiling had a red circular stain. She suspected Jennifer saw the same thing.

"Okay," Beth said.

"I'll help Beth," Jennifer said to Betsy.

Betsy turned and left, leaving Beth feeling puzzled.

Once Betsy was gone, Beth faced Jennifer.

"What was that all about?" Beth said.

"I have no idea," Jennifer said.

A moment later, a loud crash echoed from the East Wing.

Betsy paused, startled by the sound, then turned around and hurried past the restroom toward the East Wing. At the nurses' station, the noise also jolted Missy and Tammy. They sprang into motion, racing in the same direction Betsy had been seconds before.

Jennifer and Beth exited the restroom, bringing up the rear of the group.

CHAPTER 10

Betsy pushed open the door to room 115 but Missy was the first to enter. The other nurses stood outside the entrance.

"What happened?" Missy said, concerned for Jack more so than anything else.

Jack had his back against the window seal looking down at the floor.

"I thought the fluorescent bulb shattered on the ground," Jack said. He looked at all the nurses staring at him in disbelief. "What's wrong," Jack said. "Why is everyone staring at me?"

"We heard a crash," Missy said.

"Are you alright?" Tammy said.

"I'm fine," Jack said.

"It was deafening," Betsy said.

"It must've been the sto…" Jack said, but didn't finish.

A car crashed through the window as if hurled by a tornado, knocking Jack forward.

Even though the other nurses were still behind the doorway, they flinched by instinct from the imminent threat. For several stunned seconds, the nurses stared at the vehicle embedded in the building's side, unable to process how it had materialized where the window once stood. Glass fragments lay in jagged triangles across the linoleum, and the entire frame of the opening buckled and warped as though the wall had contracted around the intrusion. Steam hissed from beneath the crumpled hood, billowing up in thick, spectral clouds. The vapor was so dense it obscured the outside, transforming the world beyond into a void.

Jack lay on the floor, contorted into a grotesque position with his body only inches from being severed in half.

Missy's custom Halloween costume depicting Cavity Sam from the electronic board game Operation now wore Jack's blood. Something was wrong with her legs. Why wouldn't they move? The wetness hit her first—warm droplets that speckled her cheeks, her lips. Missy tasted copper. Salt. She stood frozen, the oversized tweezers still hanging from her neck. They dripped. Everything dripped. The yellow fabric of her costume—so bright just moments ago, so cheerful—now wore Jack's insides on the outside. The cartoon heart on her chest, once a joke about the game's buzzer mechanism, lost its humor seeing the dark stains spreading across it. Her breath came shallow. Quick. Missy's knees finally unlocked. She stumbled backward into Tammy's hands. She paused for a moment, gazing at Jack's body sprawled on the floor. She turned to face Alfred, who seemed unfazed by the surrounding chaos. In a daze, Missy stepped out of the room, and after walking about thirty feet down the hallway, she crumpled to the ground in tears. Tammy walked with Missy, steadying her back to the nurses' station.

"Say, isn't that Kate's car?" Jennifer said.

They gazed at the vehicle for a moment; an orange AMC Gremlin with a white racing stripe curling down the sides, but most of its surfaces were now stippled with flakes of concrete and glass. The passenger-side headlight was a glassy black crater, but the driver's side was intact and shone into the room, casting harsh, angular shadows that jittered with every wisp of steam.

Jennifer took a hesitant step forward, shielding her eyes from the glare. The fog was so thick, making it hard to see even the hood ornament, much less the interior of the car, but something on the windshield drew her eye. On the glass, not spider-webbed by impact, letters took the place of the condensation; forming words like a child's handwriting as if a trembling finger wiped away the moisture from the fog. The words were clear enough to read from where the nurses stood: TRICK OR TREAT, the O's little more than smeared circles, the T's splayed with long tails.

A sudden rattle from the car's engine made them all flinch. The windshield wipers jerked once, clearing a crescent of fog and giving them a brief glimpse of the cabin's interior. The driver's seat of the car appeared empty from Beth's perspective as she stood in front, peering through the windshield. However, what if someone was lying on the floor? The nurses wouldn't be able to spot a body from the front of the vehicle.

"I can't tell from here if anyone's inside the car," Beth said.

"Go see then," Jennifer said.

Just as Beth lifted her leg to step over Jack's lifeless body, the wipers jerked again. A groan emanated from somewhere deep in the engine, followed by the soft tick of cooling metal.

"That's definitely Kate's car," Jennifer said.

For a moment, the only movement was the ceaseless drift of steam, the slow, downward crawl of condensation on the glass. Then, the letters on the windshield began to bead and run, little tears of water gathering at the bottoms of each letter. The message blurred, but did not disappear.

With caution, Beth approached the wreckage, careful to step over the oozing spill of Jack's blood, which had pooled around the shattered glass, a glistening black syrup clinging to the cracks in the linoleum. She kept her gaze locked on the Gremlin's driver's side door. She peered through the shattered glass and, for a fleeting moment, caught a glimpse of her own reflection where a window should have been. To heighten the unease, she noticed a shape move behind her. Startled, she jerked upright; her heart battered her chest from the inside. She turned and looked behind her but found no one there. She felt a sudden chill; the tiny hairs on her arms stood erect.

The other nurses noticed Beth flinch.

Jennifer's jaw stiffened, her lips pressed into a line.

"What's wrong?"

"What did you see?" Tammy said.

Beth forced a smile, shook her head, and turned again to the car. She took a shuddering breath and leaned closer, peering through the aperture of mangled glass. She swept her gaze over the rest of the interior. The smell of Wrigley's spearmint gum hung in the air like a dangling air freshener. Chewing gum wrappers covered the floor mats. She spotted a floral-print umbrella on the floor of the passenger side and wondered why Kate hadn't expected rain.

"There's no one here," Beth said, her voice barely rising above the rumble of rain against the building's exposed wall.

"Get back over here before something else happens," Betsy said.

Beth took a cautious step back, feeling the crunch of glass beneath her shoe. She almost slipped on a pool of blood, but caught herself and regained her balance. She made her way to the others, but before she took her first step, she noticed something unusual out of the corner of her eye.

"Judging from the heat coming from the car, I'd guess Kate used her remote start to warm it up," Betsy said.

Tammy reappeared, her face slack with shock, but her hands steady. She hovered at Betsy's elbow; eyes locked on the car.

"Only a tornado could lift a car and toss it through the window," Tammy said. "Wouldn't you agree?"

"You're right," Jennifer said, with her arms folded across her stomach. "That means Kate never left."

"If it weren't for the storm, I'd suspect someone picked her up and she planned to return for her car later," Betsy said.

"Sounds like you've had experience with that situation," Jennifer said.

"Not I," Betsy said. "I love my husband; he's my best friend. But I know others who marry for security and would cheat on their man just to satisfy their self-centered, miserable lives."

"It makes little sense," Tammy said.

"What do you mean?" Betsy said.

Tammy pointed a trembling finger at the Gremlin's windshield, at the fog-wiped words that had blurred and bled down the glass. "Why would she write that on the windshield?"

"Not to mention, why would she leave her car running while she went off with someone else?" Jennifer said.

"Maybe someone broke into the car and left that message," Betsy said, but the explanation didn't satisfy even her.

Alfred stirred.

"Could I have another blanket?" Alfred said through half-slit eyes. "I feel a chill."

Alfred went right back to sleep, not any wiser to Jack's eyeball resting on his right arm as if watching him rest. Despite the car being half inside his room and half outside, Alfred continued to snore. Water splashed against the rear of the vehicle, which extended beyond the building.

"Beth, I want you to roll Alfred's bed to room 121, where Roland Ditmeyer lay in a coma. And grab him a fresh warm blanket." Betsy said, tilting her head toward Alfred.

"Alright," Beth said. "What if he wakes up?"

"I don't think you need to worry yourself with that?" Betsy said. "If he does, just explain there's been a leak in his room, and he's being moved."

"Got it," Beth said, releasing all the brakes and moving Alfred when Tammy stopped her, removed Jack's eyeball from Alfred's arm, then nodded for Beth to proceed.

Betsy drew the cubicle curtain to create a barrier around the vehicle in the first part of the room. "It's not much, but it's the best we can manage for now," Betsy said.

"What should we do with Jack?" Tammy said.

"We need to lay him on a blanket in the walk-in freezer," Betsy said.

"In the freezer?" Jennifer said.

"Well, we can't just leave him here," Betsy said. "Unless you want to smell the stench of his decomposing body wafting down the hall and have to explain to the residents where the horrendous smell is coming from."

"The freezer works," Jennifer said, nodding in agreement.

"Not to change the subject, but don't you think it's odd that we all heard the crash before it actually happened?" Tammy said.

"Yeah, I was with Beth when we heard it," Jennifer said. "The timing doesn't make sense."

"I was talking with Missy," Tammy said. "The sound had come as if it had come from the future."

Jennifer nodded, but she didn't meet anyone's eyes. She fidgeted with her sleeve, her nails worrying a loose thread. "Beth and I were down the hall when we heard it. Then we walked over and—" She bit the inside of her cheek, as if she could chew through her own uncertainty. "It was like the crash waited for us. Like it needed an audience."

Betsy's eyes narrowed, her brow furrowing over a thousand unfinished thoughts.

"It was as if we were meant to see this incident as it happened."

"What, like promoters shoot off a firework to signal the show will begin in thirty minutes, summoning us to the event?" Tammy said.

"Something like that," Betsy said.

They exchanged glances for a moment.

"I'll go and grab the stretcher," Tammy said.

Just as she exited the room, the lone headlight on Kate's vehicle extinguished, plunging the well-lit space into darkness.

CHAPTER 11

As Beth approached room 121, she heard a young girl's voice singing. She listened.

JESUS LOVES ME, THIS I KNOW, FOR THE BIBLE TELLS ME SO; LITTLE ONES TO HIM BELONG, I AM BLESSED FOR HE IS STRONG. YES, JESUS LOVES ME. YES, JESUS LOVES ME. YES, JESUS LOVES ME. THE BIBLE TELLS ME SO.

Beth smiled and knocked on the door.
"Nurse," Beth said.
Upon entering, she found Roland Ditmeyer, a 32-year-old man, lying in a coma. Bandages covered the burns on his hands, and he was on a ventilator because of smoke inhalation.
Next to him sat a little girl in a white dress.

Beth figured her age to be at most between nine and ten.

"Hi there," Beth said. "I'm Beth. What's your name?"

"Cloreese," the little girl said, holding Mr. Ditmeyer's hand.

Cloreese noticed Beth looking at the cat resting at the foot of the bed.

"His name is Raphael," she said.

"Nice name," Beth said. "Your singing is very pretty."

"Thank you," Cloreese said.

"Where's your mommy?" Beth said.

"She's in heaven," Cloreese said.

"Oh, I see," Beth said.

"Is someone taking care of you while your daddy gets better?" Beth said.

"God watches over me," Cloreese said.

"Yes, He does," Beth said.

Cloreese smiles.

"I need to move Mr. Opus in here to keep your dad company," Beth said. "Like neighbors."

She stepped back into the hallway to fetch Alfred, rolling him in beside Roland Ditmeyer and securing the brakes. Afterward, she turned to Cloreese.

"Are you hungry? Would you like something to eat?" Beth said.

"No, thank you," Cloreese said. "I'm fine."

"Is there someone I can call?" Beth said.

"Who do you want to call?" Cloreese said.

"I guess there's not much use in trying when the phones aren't working," Beth said.

"Will you shave him?" Cloreese said.

"You want me to shave his face?" Beth said.

"Just his beard," Cloreese said. "He doesn't normally wear a beard."

"Well," Beth said.

"Please," Cloreese said.

"I suppose I could do that," Beth said.

"Thank you," Cloreese said.

"I need to get Alfred some new warm blankets first, then I'll attend to Mr. Ditmeyer, okay?" Beth said.

Cloreese nodded and smiled.

Beth grabbed a pair of scissors and a washtub. Cloreese observed as Beth began using the scissors to cut away the thick hair that had taken over Mr. Ditmeyer's face. The stubble that remained was dense and uneven. Initially, she thought she might need to borrow an electric shaver from another residence, but after rummaging through the drawers of the bureau next to Mr. Ditmeyer's bed, she found an electric razor wrapped in a paper towel left behind by a previous occupant. It had tape on it with the name BEATRICE written in block letters in black marker. Beth tipped Mr. Ditmeyer's jaw with two fingers and began working the razor across the contours of his face, removing the hair mass that had taken over his face like wild weeds until it was short enough for her to use a close-shaving razor. The more she worked, the more the man's features emerged from behind the beard: high cheekbones, a cleft in the chin, a faint scar running from the right nostril to the lip.

The girl watched, hands folded in her lap.

Beth applied shaving foam and started transforming Mr. Ditmeyer's face with each stroke. Halfway through the shave, Beth paused, for a moment recognizing this man.

I know this man, Beth thought.

Cloreese noticed Beth's reaction and smiled.

Beth swallowed. Her mouth was dry. There was a sudden pressure at her temples, a cold prickle at the base of her spine. She lifted her gaze and found the little girl watching her not with the curiosity of a child, but with an acuteness that was almost adult.

As Beth guided the razor beneath his earlobe, she felt something hard—a rosary around his neck. This rosary was unique; Beth recognized it as the one displayed at the Weather the Storm school for the blind and deaf, where she taught.

She remembered it hanging over the door, visible to those exiting the school—those who weren't blind. The rosary held no monetary value to the wealthy but was sacred to the devoted servants of God. A woman who had visited Medjugorje in Yugoslavia, a holy site for believers, had donated it. Beth couldn't recall the woman's name, only that she had passed away and left the rosary to the school. Instead of the usual ten beads for the Hail Mary prayers, the rosary featured miniature pink roses, and miniature yellow roses marked the beads for the Our Father prayers.

Beth wondered if Roland had been trying to save the rosary when the smoke from the fire knocked him unconscious, leading him here, or if the glass display case containing the rosary had fallen and struck him on the head as he entered the building.

I may never know, she thought.

Roland was a city engineer in 1966, but he had once worked as a firefighter in his youth. Beth rolled up his sleeve to examine his upper arm, where she found a tattoo depicting a firefighter's helmet encircled by four segments. The top segment read "Fire," the bottom one "Rescue," the left featured an image of a ladder, and the right displayed a fire hydrant. Crisscrossing between each section at an angle was a firefighter's axe, just like the one Roland Ditmeyer had carried years ago when she knew him, though this man appeared just as youthful as she was. It was difficult for her to comprehend this strange occurrence. After lowering his sleeve, she glanced at her clipboard for identification.

"Are you alright?" Cloreese said.

"Yes," Beth said, feeling a little unsettled.

Tiny strands of hair clung to his face. Beth gently wiped away the last remnants with a damp towel before using a dry one to dab his face, all while he lay still, unaware of the attention he was receiving.

"Well, how's that?" Beth said.

"He looks well-defined," Cloreese said. "Don't you think?"

"Yes, you're right," Beth said.

Beth carried the towels into the bathroom, raising her voice to reach Cloreese.

"If you need anything else, I'll be at the nurses' station down the hall," she said, tossing the used towels into the soiled linen collection bin. "Do you know where that is?" She said, expecting a response from Cloreese, but only silence returned to her. Stepping out of the bathroom, she added, "I'll check back later," her voice dropping to a normal level as she noticed Cloreese was gone. Beth raised her eyebrows in surprise.

As Beth exited the room, she nearly collided with Jed, who confronted her from his wheelchair.

"Oh," she said, caught off guard by the unexpected obstacle. Jed fixed his gaze on her, examining her uniform with a look of confusion, as if he were seeing a mermaid.

"You bear a striking resemblance to someone I knew back when I was about your age," Jed said.

"Is that so?" Beth said.

"Yes," Jed said. "You even sound just like her."

"Did you know her well?" Beth said.

"Well enough to care a great deal for her but not as much as I would have liked. I never got the chance," Jed said.

"Why not?" Beth said.

"She rushed into a burning building to save students, and that was the last time I saw her," Jed said.

"I'm sorry," Beth said.

"That was fifty-nine years ago," Jed said. "Right here in this very spot."

"What happened?" Beth said.

"Lightning struck the building and traveled down some electrical conduit attached to a steel I-beam to the basement, where I was checking the boiler. I was the school's janitor. I was right next to a disconnect shut-off switch when the lightning hit and blew the electric box's cover off, knocking me back onto the floor and nearly knocking me out," Jed said.

"How'd you escape the fire?" Beth said.

"A little girl grabbed my hand and shook me until I came to," Jed said. He looked down for a moment.

Beth glanced back at the room before returning her attention to him.

"Did the girl save you?" Beth said.

"Yeah," Jed said, nodding. "Funny thing is, I don't remember what happened to her."

"What do you mean?" Beth said.

"I looked toward the electric box and saw sparks shooting out from underneath it toward a thirty-gallon brown fiber drum filled with dirty greasy rags. I reached for a fire extinguisher when I caught a glimpse of two glowing peepers staring back at me from behind some pipes."

"Did you see a face?" Beth said.

"No, just those red glowing eyes," Jed said.

"Red?" Beth said.

"Yeah," Jed said.

"What happened next?" Beth said, biting at her bottom lip.

Jed noticed.

"That fiber drum caught fire, and the heat and oily smoke must've snapped me out of my daze. By then, the fire had traveled up through a vent, igniting the ceiling tiles on the second floor," Jed said. "I learned more details later on."

"Oh, my gosh," Beth said, shocked.

"It happened so fast," Jed said. "I looked around, but the little girl was gone, so I climbed the stairway, covering my face with my shirt. I knew where the exit was, so I made my way out, holding on to what little air I had left. When I finally reached the outside, I started coughing and gagging."

"Why didn't the fire alarms sound?" Beth said.

"How'd you know about that?" Jed said.

"Oh, I, I must've read about it," Beth said.

"It's true," Jed said. "The fire alarms didn't go off at first. By the time they did, it was too late; the damage was already done. The building was old and caught fire quickly. The school was underfunded, and the maintenance suffered, leading to code violations."

"That's so sad," Beth said. "I never knew."

"Why would you?" Jed said.

"Right," Beth said.

"At first, the onlookers tried to blame me," Jed said.

"Why?" Beth said.

"When I came out with my face covered in soot, they were hollering I started the fire by smoking in the basement," Jed said. "That same little girl was there again for me."

"So, she made it out?" Beth said.

"Yeah. While I was coughing and spitting out soot, there she was again. She defended me in front of the crowd, telling them she saw the lightning strike the building, which caused the fire," Jed said.

"She must've been a really brave girl," Beth said.

"I never got the chance to thank her though,"

"Why not?" Beth said.

"After all the commotion, I looked for her, but she was nowhere to be found. It was like she had disappeared into thin air," Jed said.

"What did this little girl look like," Beth said.

"She wore a white dress and shiny white shoes, had long blonde hair, and seemed to radiate a joyful aura. When the rain hit my face, covered in soot, squiggly lines ran down my cheeks like mascara tears, Jed said, but her dress and shoes were pure white."

Beth realized Jed had described Cloreese whom she had just spoken with.

At that moment, she hears a page come through.

"It's the nurses' station," Beth said. "You'll have to excuse me."

"Sure," Jed said.

He rolls his wheelchair backwards to let Beth pass.

As she walked away, she paused and turned back.

"The woman you mentioned who rushed into the burning building," Beth said.

"Her name was the same as the one on your name tag," Jed said, "Beth. She was a reading teacher, wearing the same outfit you're wearing now."

"But you said she was a schoolteacher," Beth said.

"That's right," Jed said. "On Halloween, she dressed in a nurse's costume."

"Did you see anyone help Beth?"

"Roland, the city engineer, went into the building after her," Jed said. "He seemed to be in his early thirties, but he also had vanished without a trace."

"No one ever found his remains?" Beth said.

Jed said, "Right, no one ever saw either him or Beth again. It was as if they had never existed at all."

"That's so tragic," Beth said. "We'll talk some more later."

"Sure, could use the company," Jed said.

Beth smiled and walked away.

CHAPTER 12

Missy sat wrapped in a warm blanket, her usual playful spirit gone as she sulked in her chair.

"Where were you, Beth?" Betsy said.

"I was tending to Alfred's needs when the little girl asked me to shave her dad," Beth said.

"What little girl?" Jennifer said.

"Cloreese, the little girl in room 121 sitting next to her dad, Roland Ditmeyer," Beth said.

Jennifer raised her eyebrows and glanced at Betsy.

"Did I say something wrong?" Beth said.

"He doesn't have a daughter," Betsy said.

The sharp, high-pitched buzz of the intercom panel interrupted the intense moment, causing Jennifer to jolt. Normally the buzzer never affected her, it was to be expected in her line of work but this time she felt vulnerable after being deeply engrossed in the conversation about a little girl whose origins were a mystery, who no one knew who she belonged to, how she got here, and why no one else had seen her.

"Can I help you?" Betsy said.

"This is Tammy. I was checking on John Doe when…" Tammy said.

"What?" Betsy said.

"You need to get down here, room 103," Tammy said.

"Is everything all right?" Jennifer said.

"Let's just say I've found Kate," Tammy said.

Missy, who had been silently staring at the floor, looked up and began to sob.

CHAPTER 13

The five of them—Betsy, Missy, Tammy, Jennifer, and Beth—stood in a tight semicircle around John Doe's gurney, trading glances like convicts waiting for the judge's verdict. They were contemplating their next move.

"Looks like Kate took your advice," Missy said to Jennifer.

The others stared at her as if she had lost her sanity; her tears made her mascara smudge, adding to her rattled appearance.

Beth glanced down and noticed a wedding ring on the floor. She bent down to pick it up, examining it as if to appreciate its beauty. She turned to Tammy.

"She was married?" Beth said.

"Yeah," Betsy said.

"Unhappily, now that all the evidence is out in the open so to speak," Missy said.

"Her husband had E.D.," Jennifer said.

"E.D.?" Beth said.

"You know, erectile dysfunction," Tammy said.

Missy snickered, a sound that had the brittle edge of a nervous breakdown. She bent her index finger back and forth, mimicking the movement of a cartoon worm while making a quirky, squeaky, sadistic sound reminiscent of rusty bedsprings in a cheap hotel.

"I get it," Beth said, losing her patience. "It's a shame."

"For her or her husband," Jennifer said.

"Both," Beth said.

"If she had any shame before you sure wouldn't know it now," Betsy said.

"What's that saying? You become what you hate," Tammy said.

"What do you mean?" Beth said.

Missy rolled her eyes as if the information was as common as the weather.

"Her dad raped her," she said.

"Oh my gosh," Beth said, "her biological dad?"

They all nodded in agreement.

"She couldn't forgive her father; therefore, her resentment kept her tethered to him. So, in retrospect, she became consumed with negative emotions that dominated her thoughts and actions, thus causing her to unconsciously emulate the very thing she despised," Tammy said.

"What should we do?" Beth said.

"We need to get her down and put her in the freezer with Jack," Betsy said.

"Shouldn't we take a picture first in case the police want proof? I don't want to get blamed for this," Tammy said.

"Good thinking," Jennifer said.

Betsy snapped a few pictures with her phone.

Missy smiled for a selfie with Kate hanging by her panties in the background. In one snapshot, she stuck her tongue out.

"You really didn't just do that," Tammy said.

"I'll never see her again. This will be our last picture together," Missy said.

"You want to remember her like this?" Jennifer said, pointing toward Kate.

Missy shrugged.

"Well, I'd rather be sitting next to her at a tiki bar in Barbados with little umbrellas in the drinks and hot shirtless guys behind us, but this will have to do. I don't have any pictures with her," Missy said. Besides, I'm not the one who gave her the condom."

"What, you think I'm responsible just because I gave her a condom?" Jennifer said.

"I'm just saying she wouldn't be lying here like this right now if you hadn't given it to her," Missy said.

Jennifer cut her off with a sharp wave of the hand.

"You don't know that. To me, it's obvious she wasn't thinking straight. If she were desperate enough to put her job and her marriage at risk, who knows to what extent she'd go to get her rocks off. Oh, and by the way, from now on just forget about asking to use my nail clippers, just so you know, in the chance you might use the nail file to slice your wrist."

Another thunderclap vibrated the windows, followed by a long, low rumble. The lights flickered once and held.

"I guess the storm isn't easing up any tonight," Tammy said.

"Okay, let's move her?" Betsy said, looking at Jennifer.

"Don't look at me, I'm not touching her panties," Jennifer said while making a sour face.

Beth places a pair of surgical gloves on her hands.

"I'll help," Beth said, snapped the surgical gloves into place.

"I'll go and get the stretcher," Tammy said.

CHAPTER 14

While waiting for Tammy to return with the spine board back stretcher with belts, Betsy couldn't resist the sound of the television in Ruth Bate's room across the hallway.

"Hi, I'm Michelle Piper. In tonight's local news, a boy has choked on a piece of hard candy just hours after beggars played their tricks or reaped their treats. Carrie Reed has the latest. Carrie?"

Jennifer whispered something to Beth when she paused and watched Betsy stepping out into the hallway. Betsy stood at the threshold of Ruth's room; her eyes fixed on the television mounted high on the wall.

"I'm reporting live from Lakeside Memorial Hospital, where Blake Monaghan has died from choking on a piece of Halloween candy just moments ago.

"No, Betsy," said, cried out.

"What began as a fun day of collecting treats turned tragic. The boy, identified as Blake Monaghan, was ascending a flight of stairs with a basket of laundry when the accident happened. According to reports, the family dog, Chester, was lying on the landing as Blake ascended from the basement. The Labrador Retriever tripped Blake, causing him to fall backwards, lodging the hard piece of candy in his throat. Blake's father, Roy Monaghan, attempted the Heimlich maneuver and immediately called for paramedics, but despite their best efforts, the child was pronounced dead on arrival at the hospital. Carrie Reed, back to you."

Beth's face drained of color.

Jennifer looked away.

The camera cut to an interview with a neighbor, a woman clutching a damp tissue, eyes puffy.

"He was always smiling," she stammered. "He was such a good kid. They had only got the dog last spring, but Blake loved that animal. He loved Halloween. I saw him earlier, dressed as a pirate. I—I can't believe he's gone."

Betsy felt her knees buckle beneath her. She sank to the floor, kneeling and clutching her stomach with her left hand. She clenched her palms into fists so tight the nails cut crescent moons into her skin. Air wouldn't come. Her mouth was full of sand. Her mouth was full of sand. Her mind tried, again and again, to unhear what it had heard, to erase the sounds now etched in her memory, to rewind time, to reach back and snatch Blake from the precise instant before everything went wrong. Overwhelmed with grief, she began to cry, shaking with hysteria, touching Beth and Jennifer's emotions, compelling them to rush to her side.

Missy found the remote control and switched the station to the same channel in John Doe's room.

"Coming up next: could local Halloween candies be to blame? Our investigative team digs deeper into the safety of this year's treats."

At the end of the broadcast, Missy observed the news station showing a fading image of Betsy's son before static made it disappear.

Tammy returned with the stretcher.

"What's wrong?" Tammy said.

Betsy hauled herself upright, face slick with tears, hands still trembling. She pressed her cell phone to her cheek.

"I need to talk to my husband," Betsy said while attempting to get a call through with her cell phone.

"No one has reception with this violent storm," Tammy said.

Betsy didn't even look at her. She stabbed at the phone again, her thumb trembling to the point the device shifted in her sweaty palms, but before it could slip from her grasp, she tightened her grip to keep from dropping it. She saw no bars, no signal, no hope. She needed Roy. She needed to hear his voice. Needed him to say it wasn't true, or that he'd heard nothing, or that their son was still alive.

Jennifer brushed the hair from her own eyes and said, with forced calm, "Try the landline at the nurses' station."

Betsy ran down the hallway, almost fell, righted herself, and kept running, one arm clutching her phone, the other cradling her gut.

"What did I miss?" Tammy said.

"The news broadcast reported that Betsy's son Blake died from choking. The segment just played. Betsy heard it live," Jennifer said.

"How old was he?" Tammy said.

"I believe he was twelve," Jennifer said.

"You should go be with her. Beth, Missy, and I can take care of Kate," Tammy said.

Beth nodded in agreement.

"Okay, okay," Jennifer said.

Beth assisted Tammy in maneuvering the stretcher into John Doe's room while Jennifer sprinted down the hallway to catch up with Betsy.

Betsy arrived at the nurses' station, her breath coming in quick gasps. She knocked over a cup of pens reaching for the landline phone and, without wasting a second, dialed her husband's number. The coiled cord stretched taut in her shaking hand. She listened as the line went dead after a single ring. Jennifer approached as Betsy jabbed the numbers in again. And again. With every failure, her chest grew tighter, as if she might choke just as her son had.

"What am I going to do? I've got to get ahold of Roy," Betsy said.

The television blinked to life with a distressing urgency: a test pattern, then the familiar face of meteorologist Guy Hanson. Jennifer seized the remote, turning the volume up.

"A tornado warning has been issued for these counties—" the man's finger jabbed at a weather map, already peppered with angry red and purple splotches. "Check the bottom of the screen for your county. I repeat, several tornadoes have touched down, causing severe damage. If you are in the path of this storm, take cover immediately. Get to your basement. If you don't have a basement, get in a bathtub. Avoid all areas with sharp objects, like garages or kitchens. Steer clear of windows. Again: if you are in the path of this storm, please take shelter now. As shown on the map, this storm is very large and is causing a lot of destruction. We expect it to last throughout the night and into the morning," meteorologist Guy Hanson said. The sound from the television faded, leaving the picture distorted until it too turned to static.

"I need to go home," Betsy said.

"Have you completely lost it?" Jennifer said. "Did you not just hear that guy?"

Betsy grabbed her purse and dashed down the corridor towards the exit, with Jennifer trailing behind.

As Betsy reached the inner doors, she fumbled for her car keys. Just as she was about to enter the code on the keypad, a burst of blue-white sparks leaped from the housing, stinging her hand. She recoiled at the dangerous surge of electricity, stumbling backwards and clutching her wrist. The hallway lights flickered.

Jennifer grabbed the nearest fire extinguisher and, with urgency, yanked the pin and sprayed the keypad with a blizzard of white. The powder stuck to the blackened box and drifted to the floor like snow. The scent of burned wires filled the air, and the two women heard the outer doors rattling and the wind howling. The wind had painted streaks of rain and dirt against the windows.

Betsy tried the door, but it wouldn't budge.

"That's just great," Betsy said. "We're all trapped in here."

Jennifer's hands were shaking to the point of dropping the extinguisher, but regained control and then sat it down and wiped her palms on her scrub pants.

"Better to be in here than out there," she said. "I understand what you're going through right now but we have to think about all these patients. We're under a tornado warning advisory. How can you expect to get to where you want to go without putting your life in danger? I'm sure by now, most of the streets have flooded. The only rational thing is to stay put."

She placed a palm on Betsy's shoulder and squeezed once for comfort.

Tammy, Beth, and Missy advanced together from the corridor like a single mass.

"We took care of Kate," Tammy said.

"Okay, you're right. We need to be ready for the worst-case scenario," Betsy said.

"That's that boy scout mom taking over," Missy said.

"Given that we're a long-term care facility, Beth and I will find the battery generators and place them outside the rooms of residents who rely on artificial life support, like those in comas," Betsy said. She wiped away her tears with her palm.

"Yeah, like John Doe," Tammy said.

"Exactly," Betsy said.

Beth stood behind Betsy, hands folded tight beneath her armpits. She wanted to say something, to offer comfort, but found herself speechless.

"The ventilators have emergency battery backup systems in case of a power outage," Tammy said.

"I think it's best as a precautionary measure in case one of the battery backup's faults on one of the ventilators," Betsy said.

"Also, you are aware that this building has automatic standby generators that kick on in case some drunk hits a power line or lightning strikes a transformer," Jennifer said. "Since insulin needs to be kept cold, it's crucial to maintain refrigeration."

"What if lightning strikes the generators?" Betsy said.

"What's the chance of that happening?" Jennifer said. "I mean, everyone has taken a risk taking a shower or a bath during storms, and according to analysts, there has been no record of anyone dying from lightning while taking a shower. I mean, the odds of that generator getting struck by lightning in our lifetimes are about one in fifteen thousand."

"The real question is what are you going to do if it does?" Betsy said. "Are you willing to risk these patients' lives over such improbability?"

"I'll gather up some flashlights," Missy said.

"Jennifer and I will get buckets of ice and have them ready in the walk-in freezer," Tammy said.

"Remember, no open flames such as candles due to residents using oxygen," Betsy said. "And someone should have drawn all the curtains already, but we need to double-check. If the windows break, the curtains can provide some protection against flying glass or debris."

"Of course," Jennifer said. "Thanks for staying." She squeezed Betsy's arm.

Betsy managed a half-smile.

Once alone with Tammy, Jennifer tried to lighten the tense atmosphere.

"I bet she has a solar-powered dildo," Jennifer said.

"You think there is such a thing?" Tammy said with a mischievous grin.

"If she had one, it would never see the light of day," Jennifer said.

They exchanged glances, and both giggled.

CHAPTER 15

Beth maneuvered the last of the carts loaded with the backup battery generator into place against the wall just outside of room 121, where she had last seen the little girl, Cloreese. She intended to check in on Cloreese, but before she could peek her head into room 121, she heard the little girl's voice coming not from Roland Ditmeyer's room but another room further down the hall. Beth followed the sound until she found herself outside room 117, where the nameplate read Martha Carmichael.

Beth stepped inside and spotted Cloreese seated next to Martha Carmichael's bed on the vinyl guest chair, her feet not reaching the linoleum, white shoes swinging idly.

"Well, there's a familiar face," Beth said to Cloreese.

She looked at Martha and smiled.

"Hi, Mrs. Carmichael, my name is Beth, and I will be assisting with your care this evening," Beth said.

"Please call me Martha," Martha said, clutching a rosary in her hands.

"Is there anything I can get you?" Beth said.

"No thank you," Martha said. "I'm fine."

"Cloreese, I think Mrs… I mean, Martha could use some rest," Beth said.

"Oh, please let her stay," Martha said. "She's no bother. I could really use the company."

"Well, only if you promise to protect Cloreese. She might be frightened by the storm and need some comfort. Isn't that right, Cloreese?" Beth said, winking at the little girl as if to acknowledge that it was Martha who was actually frightened, not Cloreese.

"There is no storm," Cloreese said.

A thunderclap outside begged the differ.

Beth glanced up at the ceiling, acknowledging the booming noise of the roaring menace outside. Then, she turned her gaze to Cloreese, raising her eyebrows as if to inquire whether Cloreese had heard the thunder.

"By the time your hand slaps the cheek of a resident, know that Mrs. Carmichael will have passed on," Cloreese conveyed to Beth by thought and not by mouth.

Beth's heart lurched, sending a cold pulse through her chest. The words settled in her mind with the heavy pressure of prophecy, without being spoken, muttered, or whispered. She looked at Cloreese, sure now that the girl had not said a word, yet there was no denying that the message had come from her, as if Cloreese had simply moved a piece on an invisible chessboard and Beth had no choice but to acknowledge her own checkmate.

Cloreese sat placid, confident, her shoes still swinging in patient rhythm.

Beth glanced over at Martha, curious as to whether Martha was receiving the same thoughts that Beth was. Martha Carmichael closed her eyes and recited a prayer, her lips moving but making no sound. She shifted her attention back to Cloreese, realizing the message was for her mind.

I would never strike a resident, Beth thought.

"Did you say something?" Beth said, confused, searching Cloreese's eyes for any clues to her mysterious presence.

"We will comfort each other," Cloreese said.

"Okay," Beth said, still startled by Cloreese's voice inside her head. She felt violated.

Has this girl been reported to the authorities as missing? She thought.

Beth grew increasingly uneasy, realizing that Roland didn't have a daughter, and Cloreese appeared to be freely moving around the rooms while a menacing storm raged outside, terrorizing the county. She still hadn't connected Cloreese to any parent or sibling.

"I'll check in later," Beth said. "If you need anything, just let me know."

Martha opened her eyes.

"Thank you," she said.

Beth's smile appeared to soothe Martha, but when her gaze fell on Cloreese, her expression shifted. She recalled a moment when a little girl had cried for help from a second-story window of a burning school while she ensured her class was at a safe distance on the street below. Beth had rushed back into the burning building without hesitation to save that girl. Now, she questioned whether the girl calling for help and Cloreese were one and the same, wondering if Cloreese had deliberately drawn her into the building. The thought nagged at her that Cloreese might have triggered that haunting memory. She was frightened that Cloreese had the ability to read her thoughts. The girl knew something. Beth could feel the gravity of it, the way a dog senses a tremor before anyone else. Beth left the room with more questions than answers.

CHAPTER 16

An insistent buzz at the nurses' station beckoned the call for assistance in room 121 as Beth approached the counter.

"Beth," Betsy said.

"Yes," Beth said.

"Did you place Alfred Opus in room 121 with Mr. Roland Ditmeyer?" Betsy said.

"Yes, I just came from there," Beth said. "I set the cart with the battery backup outside his room." She thought it might be wise not to mention Cloreese this time.

"Did you get him a warm blanket?" Betsy said.

"Yes," Beth said. "But that was earlier."

Betsy

Betsy appeared puzzled and raised her index finger, signaling Beth to hold on for a moment.

"Yes, can I help you?" Betsy said, answered the page for room 121 with the push of the talkback button.

Silence followed.

Betsy pressed the talkback button again.

"Mr. Opus, is that you? Do you need some help?" Betsy said.

There was no reply.

Betsy stepped out from behind the counter.

"Something's wrong," Betsy said. "We need to go check on Alfred."

Betsy took the lead, and Beth followed.

CHAPTER 17

While Betsy and Beth checked on Alfred in room 121, Jennifer, Tammy, and Missy sat at the nurses' station hoping the rest of the night would return to the usual boring routine as before.

"What do you know about Beth?" Tammy said.

"About as much as everyone else here," Jennifer said. "Why do you ask?"

"Did any of you receive an email informing you of a new hire?" Tammy said.

Jennifer shook her head. Tammy glanced at Missy, who responded with the same gesture.

"Has she done something wrong?" Missy said.

"Ever since she arrived, things have gone wrong," Tammy said.

"What, like she's brought some bad mojo with her?" Missy said.

"I'm not sure," Tammy said. "Something feels off."

"You can't blame her for the storm," Jennifer said.

Tammy appeared defeated, realizing that Jennifer had been right.

"Why does she smell like a campfire?" Missy said.

The television flickered to life, displaying an anchorman in a navy-blue suit, white shirt, and red tie, speaking into a microphone he held in his left hand.

The crawl at the bottom of the screen read: "Live Local Coverage: Tragedy at Weather the Storm Girls' School."

"In local news, a fire broke out today at the Weather the Storm girls' school for the blind and deaf, where children aged five to twelve became victims of a tragic event that has left parents seeking answers," the anchorman said. His voice was all business, but the corners of his mouth fumbled with the word 'victims.' "We'll now go to Katherine Swanson for more on this story."

The feed cut to a woman standing in a parking lot surrounded with yellow police tape, her pastel blazer appealing in contrast to the doom behind her eyes.

"Today began like any other school day for the children at the Weather the Storm girls' school for the blind and deaf, where they learned to read, write, and pray. But around ten-fifteen this morning, a fire erupted, resulting in numerous casualties. Sources indicate that the fire started in the basement, where a local teenage boy was reportedly playing with matches. Witnesses claim to have seen the janitor exiting the building just moments before the blaze ignited. Fire experts suspect that a bucket containing oily rags served as the fuel source for this devastating fire. While we may never learn all the specifics, we do know that, thanks to sixth-grade teacher Mrs. Beth Bennett, thirty students will be going home tonight to prepare for trick-or-treating, while ninety-two of their classmates and three teachers will not. This is Katherine Swanson reporting live; back to you, Ted."

The feed cut back to the anchorman, who was no longer reading from his script, but instead stared into the camera with disbelief. On the screen next to him, an image materialized: a candid photo of a woman smiling, her hair long, skin pale even in the overexposed photograph. Beneath it read: "Beth Bennett, Teacher."

"That looks just like Beth," Missy said.

"Am I correct in stating that Mrs. Beth Bennett perished in the fire?" Anchorman Ted said.

"As of right now, sources say she may have lost her life in the blaze," Katherine Swanson said. "Students have reported seeing Mrs. Bennett re-enter the burning building after ensuring her students were safe. The reason for her risking her life remains unclear. One can only speculate that perhaps her intention was to activate the fire alarm to give others a chance to escape. What is certain is that both her students and the community will remember her courage."

"We have some footage taken earlier today," Ted said. "Please be advised, I must warn the audience that some of the images you are about to see are graphic."

Raphael the cat stood in a defensive stance outside the door of room 121, staring at the entrance and hissing. Betsy found the cat's behavior peculiar. When she reached down to pick it up, the cat darted away down the hallway. Beth recalled that during her previous visit to this room, the cat had been relaxed, its tail swaying like a dust collector.

Beth shadowed Betsy as the two entered the room to find John Doe lying on a bed in the same spot she had positioned Alfred in earlier. The hairs on Beth's arms stood up, frightened by what she couldn't explain.

"Beth, I thought you said you placed Alfred Opus here next to Mr. Roland Ditmeyer," Betsy said.

"I did," Beth said.

"Then where is Mr. Opus?" Betsy said.

"I have no idea," Beth said.

As they both stared in disbelief at John Doe, the television flickered to life, displaying the same footage that Jennifer, Tammy, and Missy were watching from the nurses' station.

Beth focused her attention on the television just before she entered the burning school building, dressed in the same nurse's uniform she now wore. Puzzling as it all seems, she dressed up in a costume for Halloween in 1966 as a nurse and appeared fifty-nine years later in a nursing home. She couldn't help wondering where and when she would have ended up if she had picked a witch's costume to wear instead.

On the television, Beth saw the younger Jed approaching her on the street in front of the school to check if she was alright. She watched herself telling him to keep an eye on her class while she ran back into the building to rescue the little girl who was calling for help, even though the news broadcast had no audio of that exchange; still, Beth remembered it as if it had just happened yesterday. When Jed turned to look at the building, he saw no little girl at the window.

There's no little girl in the window, Beth thought.

Beth saw Jed reaching out to grasp her arm, attempting to prevent her from going back into the building. However, his attention redirected when a blind student named Barbara Braun stepped off the curb and almost became entangled with the hustle and bustle of oncoming traffic.

"No," Beth said, the word escaping her lips as her emotions broke through her consciousness.

She then watched as Jed intervened, grabbing Barbara's arm and guiding her back onto the sidewalk from harm's way, and felt a wave of relief wash over her. But when Jed turned back to stop Beth Bennett, it was already too late; she had dashed back into the building.

"What did you say?" Betsy said.

Beth turned away from the television to face Betsy.

"Nothing," Beth said. "I was just thinking out loud."

"Stay focused, Beth. We need to locate Alfred," Betsy said.

Oh my gosh, I hope this broadcast isn't being seen by anyone at the nurse's station, Beth thought. I'm so glad I changed my name from Bennett to Myers.

As Betsy monitored John Doe's gauges, Beth turned her attention back to the television, hoping to see what happened after she entered the building. She watched as Roland stepped through the same doorway she had just entered moments earlier. A peculiar cloud hovered above the building; unlike anything she had ever seen. Within the cloud, a red glow flickered alongside the lightning. Above the school, a single cumuliform cloud with distinct, cauliflower-like details hung, its dark shadows intertwining with illuminated white, moving like dough being kneaded and as upset as irritable bowels, while a gloomy, overcast October sky shrouded the atmosphere around the cloud and the rest of the area in the town. The fluffy, cotton-like formation hovered above the school, resembling a violent volcanic plume with sporadic red bursts, as if gases were igniting within it. Just as Roland vanished into the dense black smoke, the pyroclastic flow faded away and dissipated.

Beth regarded Roland with a look of compassion.

You're a hero, she thought.

At the nurses' station, Jennifer, Tammy, and Missy turned away from the television when the screen lost the broadcast and crackled back to static.

"Didn't that fire occur about sixty years ago?" Tammy said.

"Fifty-nine years ago, in October 1966," Jennifer said.

"How do you know that?" Missy said.

"There's a photo on the wall in the library taken a few weeks before the fire," Jennifer said.

"I never seen any photos like that in there before," Missy said.

"I noticed it when I gave Beth… the tour," Jennifer said.

"Beth again," Tammy said. "Maybe she didn't actually die in that fire."

"Listen to what you're saying," Jennifer said. "You know how absurd that sounds."

"Why is the network airing something that happened sixty years ago as if it were current news?" Missy said. "That's kind of corky don't you think?"

"Corky?" Tammy said, "Do you mean quirky?"

"Whatever," Missy said, shrugging.

"More like inane," Tammy said.

"What's the point?" Missy said.

"Ratings, greed, who knows," Tammy said. "It makes no sense to broadcast that event in the middle of the night."

"Exactly," Jennifer said.

Both Missy and Tammy looked at Jennifer.

"Right now, what could be more important than an update on the storm," Jennifer said.

The control panel for room 121 buzzed, illuminating the indicator for that room.

"Can I help you?" Tammy said.

"This is Betsy. Did any of you switch Alfred with John Doe?" Betsy said.

~ 149 ~

Tammy glanced around at her colleagues, all of whom were shaking their heads.

"No," Tammy said. "Why, what's up?"

"Well, John Doe is in the room where Beth placed Alfred," Betsy said.

Tammy raised her eyebrows in surprise.

Jennifer shook her head at Tammy.

"Where is Alfred?" Tammy said.

"I don't know, but could one of you check room 103 to see if he's there?" Betsy said.

"I'll go," Tammy said.

"Great, thanks," Betsy said.

"Just curious, Betsy, if you have two patients in the same room and both are in comas, who paged the nurses' station?" Tammy said.

"Whoever can answer that question might be able to tell us how John Doe got in this room with no help?" Betsy said.

"Seems kind of spooky, don't you think?" Tammy said.

"Yeah, give you something to ponder while you check on room 103," Betsy said over the intercom.

"Thanks," Tammy said with a sarcastic tone as she exited the nurses' center.

CHAPTER 18

The high winds howled outside. Jennifer wondered what kind of destruction awaited her outside. She pictured tree limbs strewn about and street signs mangled. She hoped that the roof would remain intact.

Tammy met Betsy and Beth back at the nursing station.

"Alfred is sound asleep in room 103," Tammy said.

Beth's mind seemed to be elsewhere, replaying recent events in her mind. She recalled the time she had brought flowers to her classroom, intending for the sighted students to have something beautiful to look at while the blind students could enjoy the pleasant scent. She suspected Jed thought the fireman who visited her class to discuss fire safety had given her the flowers, because the following day, she found a box of chocolates on her desk where the flowers had been, which was moved closer to the trash can. She caught a glimpse of Jed peeking through the little window in the classroom door for a second before he moved away in a hurry. Beth wanted to chase after him to thank him for the chocolates, but she couldn't leave her class unattended.

"What about you, Beth?" Tammy said.

"Sorry, I didn't hear the question," Beth said.

"Is there any romance in your life?" Tammy said.

"There's no one," Beth said.

"Ever?" Jennifer said.

"I've never been with a man," Beth said.

They all fell silent for a moment, staring at Beth as if expecting her to reveal she was kidding, but she wasn't.

"I don't want to settle," Beth said. "I want Mr. Right."

"Don't we all?" Jennifer said.

Missy noticed Betsy's mind wasn't in the conversation.

"What's going on, Betsy?" Missy said.

"We were all moving about, positioning the carts in the hallway," Betsy said.

"Yeah, that's right," Jennifer said.

"How did John Doe manage to get past this station without any of us noticing?" Betsy said.

"That was the same thing I was thinking," Jennifer said.

"Strange as it might be, it actually worked out better for us. If one of the residents' ventilators fails, we can have both residences share the same ventilator," Betsy said.

"Did you notice anything else out of place or unusual?" Jennifer said.

"Well, now that you mention it," Betsy said. "Raphael was lying outside the room, hissing, and when I tried to pick him up, he ran down the hallway as if he wanted nothing to do with that room."

"Yeah, and what's odd is that when I was in the room earlier shaving Mr. Roland Ditmeyer, that cat was sitting at the foot of his bed, purring," Beth said.

"Maybe we're situated over a ley line," Tammy said.

"A what?" Betsy said.

"A ley line," Tammy said.

"I've heard about those," Jennifer said. "You know, like how the pyramids in Egypt line up with Stonehenge on a map. They say there are some invisible pathways."

"Yeah," Tammy said, "like the Coral Castle, which is said to have magical or supernatural qualities. A guy built that out of coral, with sections weighing tons, and he did it all by himself—no crane involved."

"Really?" Betsy said. "I'd like to see that."

"Maybe this land is cursed," Missy said.

"Now you're making it sound like the Bermuda Triangle, where people, boats, and planes just vanish," Betsy said.

"Maybe we've already disappeared, and we just don't realize it yet," Missy said.

"I think some of the disappearances have been explained. I think, like bubbles rising from the ocean floor can make a boat sink," Tammy said.

"If I'm not mistaken, those who disappeared in the Bermuda Triangle reported a storm before they're not heard from again, do they not?" Betsy said.

"Not just any storm; it's a violent storm with electrical activity," Jennifer said.

"Just like the one we have tonight," Beth said.

They all paused for a moment, exchanging glances.

"I could really use a cup of coffee," Betsy said.

"I believe the machine is out of order," Jennifer said, hoped to shield everyone from the gruesome sight she had witnessed.

"Since when?" Tammy said.

"I tried earlier with no luck," Jennifer said.

Betsy recalled bumping into Jennifer in the hallway and how she had commented on how Jennifer appeared as if she had seen a ghost.

She's hiding something from us all, she thought. Maybe this is her way of warning us, to keep us safe.

Not wanting to prolong the conversation, Jennifer's gaze wandered before settling on a yellow sticky note attached to the side of the computer monitor.

Betsy followed Jennifer's gaze and peeled off the sticky note.

Please check Baxter Evans's temperature in room 113.

"I don't remember seeing this here before," Betsy said.

Lacking experience, Beth was eager to prove her usefulness by taking on any tasks, even those that the others detested doing. She could sense from their reactions that nobody wanted to do it.

"I'll take care of it," Beth said.

They all stared at her as if she had just promised to cover their mortgages for the entire year.

"Go ahead," Betsy said.

Beth picked up the medical thermometer from the desk and walked off.

They exchanged pleased looks among themselves.

At the same time, Betsy was considering a trip to the vending machines. Her desire to uncover what had frightened Jennifer was overwhelming her.

CHAPTER 19

In room 113, Baxter Evans was sound asleep when Beth entered, eager to take his temperature. At his bedside she stood.

"Mr. Evens," Beth said, "I'm Beth and I'm going to take your temperature."

Although there was some movement under his eyelids, he did not respond to her voice. He didn't even twitch his eyebrows, which some patients do before waking. She slid the oral rod into his mouth and waited for the beep. As she observed the digital display, the numbers climbed to one hundred, then one hundred and two, and finally one hundred and three. Concerned, Beth pressed the call button to alert the nurses' station.

"Can I help you?" Betsy said.

"This is Beth. The thermometer's reading is now climbing to one hundred and four," Beth said.

"The batteries are probably dying," Betsy said. "Hold tight; I'll bring some new ones."

The digital screen read one hundred five when Betsy entered the room—two points above the upper limit of her previous reading, and four beyond what any man should endure.

"It's reading one hundred and five," Beth said.

"Relax," Betsy said.

She took the thermometer from Beth and swapped out the old batteries for new ones. Keeping the probe in Baxter's mouth, Betsy powered the device back on. The screen displayed one hundred and eight degrees.

"This can't be right," Betsy said.

Betsy buzzed the nurses' station.

"Yes," Missy said.

"Missy, this is Betsy. I'm in Room 113. Could you bring me the forehead thermometer?"

"Sure, be right there," Missy said.

While waiting for Missy to arrive, Betsy moved the rod in Baxter's mouth. A puff of smoke escaped his lips, as if he'd held in a draw from a cigarette; yet, according to his chart, he had never smoked.

Betsy's forehead creased in confusion. Missy came in and handed the thermometer to Betsy. She aimed the device at Baxter's forehead and pulled the trigger, and the screen displayed a temperature of one hundred and eight, unwavering, like a stuck car alarm in the night.

"Wow," Missy said. "That's the maximum temperature the thermometer will read. Never seen that before."

Betsy shook Mr. Even's shoulder trying to get him to respond.

"Mr. Even's can you hear me?" Betsy said.

"Beth, prepare the tub with some ice," Missy said. "We've got to get his temperature down."

Beth started to leave when Baxter opened his mouth wide. Smoke billowed out like the top of a chimney on a blazing fireplace.

"Oh my gosh," Beth said to no one and everyone.

"Forget the ice, grab a fire extinguisher," Betsy said.

"Follow me. I know where to go," Missy said to Beth.

Missy ran out of the room with Beth trailing.

Betsy yanked open Baxter's gown and examined his chest. His sternum broke through to his chest cavity with ease, releasing more smoke from his body. His fragile chest collapsed like scorched paper crumbles. His bones collapsed inward like the brittle ribs of a burned-out house. She jerked the sheet off the bed and ran to the restroom. There, she soaked a cloth in cold water under the faucet. Rushing back to Baxter, she draped the wet sheet over his flaming body, making it cling, resembling a mummy's wrappings. The water hissed into steam as it touched the burning flesh. Just then, Missy burst back into the room, extinguisher under her arm, followed by Beth clutching a second. The two women flanked the bed, eyes watering from the thick haze. The room was filling up with smoke. It was all Betsy could do to keep from gagging to think she was inhaling someone's burning flesh. She bolted into the hallway to catch her breath. Missy hurried to the side of the bed closest to the window while Beth took the opposite side.

Beth recalled a day in 1966 when a fireman had come to her classroom with a fire extinguisher, eager to demonstrate its use. It had been a refreshing break from the usual lessons, and she noticed the students were engaged, eager to learn the acronym P.A.S.S. that the fireman had written on the chalkboard. P.A.S.S. stands for Pull the pin, Aim the nozzle, Squeeze the trigger, and Sweep the extinguisher from side to side.

Missy fumbled with the unfamiliar pin in desperation, her eyes blinking away tears. "I can't—," she said.

Betsy came back in.

"Go get some air," she said to Missy.

Missy passed the extinguisher to Betsy and stumbled out into the corridor, doubling over and coughing into her sleeve.

Betsy aimed at Baxter's chest and squeezed. The foam erupted in a thick white spray, coating the body and the bed in a snowy drift. The sheet, now soaked and saturated with extinguished residue, clung to the patient's form like a death shroud. Through it, Betsy could see the distinct deflation of Baxter's torso, the collapse of organs, the shrinking of mass as the fire consumed everything within. The sheet Betsy threw over the body wasn't even discoloring. It held its bleached-white color.

"I don't see any fire," Beth said, shouted over the sound of Betsy's spraying. "It's just smoke."

Betsy stopped and looked at Beth then back at Baxter. In the short time Beth had known Betsy; she'd never seen her so frightened. Betsy was coughing, and the room's lights illuminated the smoky haze. Betsy's hands shook as she lowered the extinguisher. Over the years working as a nurse, not just here at this facility but elsewhere, she has seen deaths in every imaginable form—overdoses, gunshots, drownings, automobile accidents—but this was new. And, in some way, she knew it would never leave her.

"Go get some fresh air," Betsy said. "Have Missy find a couple of fans to draw this smoke out."

Beth nodded and left the room.

For a moment, Betsy stood alone.

Tammy peeked into the room.

"What happened?" she said.

"We were checking his temperature, and he started burning from the inside out," Betsy said.

"You mean like spontaneous human combustion?" Tammy said.

"Well, I've witnessed nothing like this myself, but if I had to guess… then… I'd say this had all the indications of it," Betsy said.

Once Missy and Beth positioned the fans to clear the thick air from the room, Betsy peeled back the wet sheet, careful not to upset what remained of the patient. The torso had collapsed, a shallow basin of chalky dust, but the flesh at the margins was untouched; the socks on his feet were still clean, the legs still plump and lifelike.

"Oh my gosh," Jennifer said, covering her nose with her right hand. "What happened? His body looks charred."

Missy and Beth joined Jennifer by the bedside, staring in disbelief.

"I read about a woman in Paris who burned up while sleeping, but the straw mattress she was sleeping on was unmarred by the fire," Tammy said.

"What is spontaneous human combustion?" Beth said."

"It's when the body ignites from within with no external flame," Betsy said. "And while the torso turns to ash like Mr. Baxter here, the head and limbs remain intact."

"If I recall correctly, there was a case in Ireland where a man, who the coroner declared dead, recorded spontaneous combustion as the official cause," Tammy said.

"I saw a documentary where a lady in northern London whose upper body enveloped in flames right in front of her parents." Betsy said, "The wooden chair she was sitting on did not burn."

"The coroner is going to have a lot of questions in the morning," Jennifer said. "Hopefully, this storm won't linger, leading the relief nurses to call off and forcing us into working overtime."

"If this keeps up, we're going to run out of room in the freezer," Tammy said.

"Look at the bright side," Missy said. "It's been a few hours, maybe Jack and Kate have frozen enough for us to start stacking the bodies."

"What is wrong with you?" Jennifer said.

"We all know you had feelings for Jack," Betsy said, "but we need you to hold it together. Don't let this night drive you off the deep end. Fight it. When the sun rises, it will be a brand new day. Okay?"

Missy nodded.

"If we're being honest, Kate would probably thank us for sandwiching her between two men," Tammy said.

Betsy rolled her eyes.

"It gives me chills just thinking about those bodies being in the freezer all night," Jennifer said.

"We might need to cook some food to create more space," Missy said.

"It'll be alright; we just have to weather the storm," Betsy said.

"Just like the sign reads outside," Jennifer said.

"That's right," Betsy said.

"I'll go and get the stretcher," Tammy said.

The others remained in the hallway to let the stench clear out.

CHAPTER 20

After putting Mr. Evans' body in the walk-in freezer, the women settled into the plush chairs at the nurses' station. Jennifer's butt had little time to enjoy the comfort of the chair when the nurses' call system chimed, signaling that room 119 needed assistance, followed by a blinking LED light.

"Yes, Rosslyn," Jennifer said. "What can I do for you?"

"I've been pressing this button for what feels like an hour," Rosslyn said.

"We've been a little busy tonight," Jennifer said.

"Well, you need to come down here," Rosslyn said.

"Straighten up, Dick," Jennifer said.

"It's Rosslyn," he said. "Mr. Winters to you."

Jennifer released the button so Rosslyn wouldn't hear her get the last word in.

"Mr. Frozen prick," Tammy said.

"That's the only way it's going to get hard," Jennifer said.

The women erupted into laughter.

As Jennifer stepped away from the station, another buzzer sounded. This time, the call indicator light was flickering on the board for room 121. The noise persisted for a moment, and Missy, Tammy, and Beth turned to Betsy, who was nearest to the central monitor console, curious why she hadn't responded to the call.

"Betsy, are you going to answer that?" Tammy said.

"Shhh," Betsy said, quieting the others as she listened intently.

The buzzer had a different tone this time. The nurses exchanged surprised and puzzled glances.

"It's Morse code," Betsy said. "Blake had to learn it for Boy Scouts, and I helped him practice. Quick, hand me that sticky notepad."

Beth grabbed the yellow notepad Betsy was pointing toward and tossed it to her. Betsy jotted down the letters.

"What does it say?" Missy said.

A long dash, followed by a dot dash dot, then two dots, then a long dash, a dot, a long dash, a dot, and finally a long dash and a dot, then a long dash again.

Once Betsy finished writing the message, the buzzer ceased. She looked up in disbelief.

"What's wrong?" Tammy said.

"It keeps repeating," Betsy said.

"What keeps repeating?" Missy said.

"Trick or treat," Betsy said.

"So who's playing a prank?" Tammy said.

"That's the strange part," Betsy said. "It's coming from bed-B in room 121."

"That's Mr. Roland Ditmeyer's room," Beth said.

"Right, and bed-B is John Doe," Betsy said.

"How can that be?" Missy said. "They're both in comas."

"Beth," Betsy said.

"Yeah," Beth said.

"You mentioned a little girl earlier," Betsy said.

"Her name is Cloreese," Beth said.

"And where did you last see her?" Tammy said.

"Room 117," Beth said.

"That's Martha Carmichael's room," Missy said.

"Yes, that's correct," Beth said. "Why do you ask?"

"Well, it seems to me we might have a little prankster on our hands," Betsy said.

"What?" Beth said.

"How else can you explain John Doe being moved when you said you didn't move him, or the call system going off for someone who can't even wiggle his toes or scratch his butt?" Betsy said.

"Are you telling me that none of you have ever seen a little girl wearing a white dress, white glossy shoes, with long blonde hair around here before?" Beth said.

They all exchanged glances and shook their heads.

"Perhaps you have an imaginary friend," Missy said.

"That's unfair," Beth said, her voice louder than intended. "It's rude and inappropriate. Furthermore, if you expect me to believe a ten-year-old little girl is going to know Morse code and have the strength or the means to relocate a man right under our noses without any of us seeing or hearing him being moved? That's what I call stretching the imagination."

"Where did you work before coming here?" Tammy said.

"I just graduated from college. My resume should still be in the office if you want to check," Beth said, lying.

"The office is locked," Tammy said.

"Look, I may not have the experience you all have, but at least I'm making a valiant effort to care for these people who need our help, despite the anomalies occurring tonight. And if I may say so, blaming me for all these strange occurrences is childish, unproductive, and frankly distasteful. You may not like me, and I might not have all the answers, but I have what it takes to survive this night. If you want to work together as a team, then you need to grow a pair of ovaries, stop pointing fingers, and show me some respect, just as I have shown you," Beth said.

They all stared at her for a moment.

Tammy opened her mouth, but before she could speak, Betsy cut her off.

"You're right," Betsy said.

Missy nodded in agreement.

"I like the part about growing a pair of ovaries," Tammy said. "I've never heard that one used before."

They all laughed.

"So, Beth," Betsy said, "tell us something about yourself."

"Well, like all of you, my name was given to me in honor of my grandmother," Beth said.

They exchanged glances and nodded, except for Betsy.

"How did you know that?" Tammy said.

"Lucky guess, I suppose," Beth said.

"I wasn't named after my grandmother," Betsy said.

"You weren't," Jennifer said.

"Nope," Betsy said.

"Who were you named after?" Missy said.

"No one; it's just a name," Betsy said.

"Like a name you'd give to a dog, cat, or car," Missy said.

Betsy fell silent. Whatever—was the expression that captured her feelings as she rolled her eyes the way a teenager will when reminded to tidy up their room or else lose their phone. Betsy redirected her focus back to Beth.

"Fresh out of school and now a nurse," Betsy said.

"You could say that," Beth said.

"Did you learn any exciting new medical breakthroughs you'd care to share?" Tammy said.

"Boring," Missy said. "I'd rather hear some scary stories." She held up her book as a reminder to everyone of what she had brought.

"I'm sure each of you has a tale or two to tell about off the wall happenings around Halloween," Beth said.

"The one thing that comes to mind is there used to be a school in this very spot that burned down," Jennifer said.

"Yeah, that's pretty creepy," Tammy said.

"We just witnessed first-hand a man burn from the inside out," Betsy said. "What can be more bizarre than that?"

"Someone returning from the dead," Beth said.

"What, like a zombie?" Tammy said.

"No, not a zombie," Beth said.

"Do you know someone who has returned from the dead?" Jennifer said.

Missy set her book back on the counter, considering the lack of interest now that Beth had drawn their attention.

"Okay, there was a man named Smith Wigglesworth. He was a British evangelist who assisted in miracles, including, believe it or not, raising someone from the dead," Beth said.

"Impossible," Tammy said.

"Actually, he raised fourteen people from the dead, one of whom was his wife, Polly," Beth said. "He believed that sickness and disease were living evil spirits. Neither he nor his wife would allow doctors or medicine into their home, as he had complete faith in divine healing. At eighty-one, he still had all his teeth with no decay. He died at eighty-seven, and the cause was simply old age."

"So does that mean children have demons if they're sick?" Missy said.

"According to his beliefs, children are not exempt," Beth said.

"In fact, I once heard a preacher say that in the book of Genesis, 9:24, when Noah awoke from his drunkenness and found out that his youngest son,

Ham, had seen him naked, Noah cursed Ham's sons and daughters, declared they would be slaves to Ham's brothers."

"So, did Ham have a dark complexion?" Missy said.

"The three sons were Shem, Ham, and Japheth; Ham was black, Shem was white, and Japheth was Asian."

"So, a demon of lust could transfer to a son or daughter from a parent, potentially leading to disease?" Tammy said.

"You've all heard of genetic diseases where a mutated gene is inherited from parent to child," Beth said. "Every time you go to the doctor's office to be seen, they want to know what diseases your parents have. So, in a sense, the offspring inherit their parents' sins, and if those sins are not exonerated, the bloodline may carry the same disease."

"Interesting," Betsy said.

"So, this Smith Wigglesworth is not a fictional character you just made up?" Tammy said.

"No," Beth said. "What I shared about him is what I learned."

"I think it's odd the way Jack died," Missy said.

"Why is that?" Beth said.

"Jack told me yesterday that he had a near miss—that he was almost involved in a bad car accident that most likely would have ended his life," Missy said.

"What did he say happened?" Tammy said.

"He mentioned he was at a red light that turned green, but instead of rushing into the intersection, something urged him to wait. He hesitated for a moment, delaying his acceleration, and it turned out to be a wise decision. A woman was texting on her phone and didn't even slow down as she sped through the red light," Missy said.

"That's freaky," Betsy said.

"Yeah, and yet he still died from a vehicle colliding with him," Missy said.

"I had a frightening experience," Jennifer said.

"What happened?" Beth said.

"When I was fourteen, I was ice skating on a frozen pond and fell through the ice. Thankfully, my dad was there to rescue me," Jennifer said.

"I was about thirteen when I had a close call. We had an electric organ plugged into an extension cord, and I wanted to use that extension cord to plug a fan in for my bedroom to help me sleep.

When I tried to unplug it, it wouldn't come free, so I attempted to use my teeth," Tammy said.

"Oh, no," Betsy said.

"Yeah," Tammy said. "I thought the other end was unplugged. I felt a tingle on my lips just before my mother rushed over to the outlet and unplugged the connection."

"You could've been electrocuted," Beth said.

"Yeah, my lips felt numb for a little while," Tammy said.

Betsy stood up.

"Where are you going?" Tammy said.

"Room 117," Betsy said. "I want to find that little girl."

"But we're about to read some scary stories from the book I brought," Missy said.

"Go ahead," Betsy said. "I've had enough scares for one night."

"And the night isn't over yet," Tammy said.

CHAPTER 21

Jennifer strolled into room 119, hesitant to turn on the light until she understood what was so urgent. She hoped the request was simple and his burden light.

I'll just be in and out, she thought. He probably just wants some water or ice, maybe a warm blanket—perhaps even the cyanide I saw in the vending machine, she joked to herself.

She aimed for the slightest chance he might go back to sleep after she tended to his needs. She wanted to avoid any bright lights that might jolt him into staying up the rest of the night barking orders for this or that.

"Mr. Rosslyn Winters, you need some...," Jennifer's voice raised an octave just as her legs slipped out from beneath her, landing her butt on the floor.

Once the others heard Jennifer's girlish scream, they came running to check on her.

Tammy switched on the light. She, like the others, discovered Jennifer sitting in a pile of wet human feces, which horrified her. When the smell hit their noses, it was the foul odor that took their breath away. To make matters worse, at the head of the bed, propped up on a mound of pillows, Rosslyn was laughing. Beth's jaw dropped, and Tammy's eyes widened at the unsettling sight of Jennifer covered in excrement.

"What happened?" Tammy said.

"Help me up," Jennifer said.

Tammy grabbed a towel from the bathroom.

"Here, grab this end," Tammy said, offering one side to Jennifer while holding the other with a firm grip. Jennifer followed Tammy's lead.

"One, two, three," Tammy said.

Tammy pulled as Jennifer used the edge of the bed for leverage to stand up. She extended her arms away from her sides, like someone who has wet paint on their hands and is cautious about touching anything.

"I called for help, but no one came," Mr. Winters said.

"So, you decided just to crap on the floor?" Jennifer said.

"We were a little busy, Missy said.

"I didn't want to lie in it," Mr. Winters said.

"You didn't warn her about the mess either, did you?" Missy said. "You let her step in it."

"If you could make it this far, you certainly could've made it to the restroom on your own," Jennifer said.

"I had help," Mr. Winters said.

"Who?" Tammy said.

"Who helped you?" Missy said.

"I don't know," Mr. Winters said. "It was dark. He had some sort of military lights on his head, a soft red glow. Not very bright—like the kind they use in combat to read a map at night."

"He?" Missy said.

"Red?" Beth said.

"Yeah, and he only helped me to the edge of the bed, no further he said, I don't know why," Mr. Winters said.

"There's no male nurse on duty tonight," Tammy said.

Mr. Winters shrugged.

A silence fell. No one wanted to be the first to suggest what they were all thinking: that there was someone in the hospital tonight who shouldn't be.

Jennifer looked down at her soiled white stockings, which were held up by a delicate lace garter belt. She pivoted her hips slowly, trying to survey the mess on her backside. The feces had ruined her sexy white nurse's costume. Once the stench became too overwhelming, she gagged, doubled over, and—without warning—vomited what she had left from her stomach onto Mr. Winter's feet. She heaved, body convulsing in violent waves, until her eyes streamed with tears. Her retro white nurse's cap with a red plus sign shifted out of place.

"Hey, stop it," Mr. Winters said. "Barf somewhere else."

"I guess she was sick of your crap," Tammy said.

Jennifer used the clean end of the towel to cover her nose as she side-stepped toward the door with the cautious choreography of a landmine technician until she reached the hallway. There was nothing left of her usual composure. The woman, who prided herself on perfection, now stood desecrated, humiliated, and half-cocked but holding back the impulse to strike the old man's face, shoving handfuls of feces into his nostrils, ears and mouth until she felt satisfied. She imagined herself allowing her tears to flow as they pleased while screaming in vengeance as she carried out the act.

Tammy covered her nose with her left hand, turned around, and walked out, with Missy and Beth following suit.

"Hey, are you going to clean this up? It stinks in here," Mr. Winters said.

"You dealt it, you smell it," Missy said and walked out the door.

Once outside the room, Tammy turned to Jennifer.

"Go clean yourself up. We'll handle this," Tammy said.

"I'll try to round up some scrubs from the lounge," Missy said.

Beth stood by for support, ready to assist.

CHAPTER 22

Tammy returned to the nurse's station and caught Beth's eye.

"Grab a bucket of hot soapy water, some towels, and a diaper," she said.

Missy, perched on the edge of the rolling chair and picking at the cupcake liner, snorted. Her eyes didn't leave the candy eyeball stared back at her from its slow descent into buttercream frosting, embedded as if in quicksand.

"You're putting him in a diaper?"

"No, Beth is," Tammy said.

Beth felt everyone's gaze pass over her, a momentary, collective assessment. She shrugged.

"Sure, no problem," she said, and meant it—this was not the worst thing the day had offered up.

"Hey if he wants to behave like a baby, he needs to be treated like one," Missy said.

"Where's Jennifer?" Beth said.

"She's taking a shower," Tammy said.

"She'll need fresh scrubs," Beth said.

"I'll help Beth, Missy said.

"I'll bring Jennifer the scrubs," Tammy said.

The call light from Mr. Winters' room flashed repeatedly. Missy muted it, but the light continued to blink. When a moment had lapsed and she was ready, she answered.

"Yes, Mr. Winters?"

"I need something for nausea," he said. "The smell is getting to me."

"That's methane gas, Mr. Winters, so make sure there're no open flames. Remember the rules, no smoking," Missy said.

"Very amusing," Mr. Winters said. "The doctor will hear about this tomorrow."

"All nurses are currently assisting other residents. All calls will be handled in the order in which we receive them," Missy said. "A healthcare provider will attend to you when one becomes available." She silenced the call again.

CHAPTER 23

Betsy peeked into Room 117. Martha Carmichael lay still beneath her thin blanket, breathing steadily. Scanning the shadows for any sign of the little girl, Betsy found nothing and backed out without causing a stir.

With the nurses' lounge just up ahead, the memory of Jennifer's pale face and wide-eyed nagged at her, remembering how scared Jennifer looked when Jennifer collided with her.

"Oh my gosh, Jennifer, you look like you just saw a ghost. Actually, you look as pale as one."

Then, to add to Betsy's curiosity when she mentioned she could really use a cup of coffee, Jennifer said in haste that the machine was out of order. Betsy decided to have a look for herself.

The canteen door swung open with a familiar squeak. Everything looked normal. Betsy stood in front of the coffee machine. She pressed the button for regular, watched the paper cup drop and fill. Taking a cautious sip, she surveyed the room. Vending machines stood fully stocked, their colorful wrappers bright behind glass. Nothing unusual.

Why would Jennifer lie about the machine being broken, she thought.

She took another sip and stepped back into the hallway.

While she retreated to the nurses' station, Betsy glanced from room to room searching for Cloreese.

A glow from Room 104 caught her attention. Inside, Tess McMillan sat motionless, her eyes fixed on the television's dancing static. When Betsy stepped into the doorway, the elderly woman didn't blink or turn—just continued staring at the screen as if Betsy weren't there at all.

"Hi Mrs. McMillan," Betsy said. "Is there anything I can get you?"

Tess's gaze remained fixed on the television.

Betsy circled the bed to Tess's right side, spotting a thin crimson line trailing from her nostril to her upper lip. She plucked two tissues from the nearby box and dabbed at the blood. Without warning, Tess's fingers clamped around Betsy's wrist with startling strength.

"Mrs. McMillan," Betsy said. "It's me, Betsy."

Her grip loosened, replaced by a warm smile.

"Hi, Betsy," Tess said.

The vacant stare had vanished, as if she were sleeping with her eyes open and now, she's fully awake and acknowledging Betsy's presence. The change in Tess's persona convinced Betsy that Tess had no memory of just grabbing her.

"You're up late tonight," Betsy said.

"Star Light, Star Bright," Tess said.

"First star I see tonight," Betsy said.

"I wish I may, I wish I might," Tess said.

"Have this wish I wish tonight," Betsy said.

They both smiled, and together they laughed.

Tess's gaze drifted to the silver-framed photograph of her husband on her nightstand.

Betsy noticed the hurt in Tess's eyes.

"How long were you married?" Betsy said.

"Fifty-three wonderful years," Tess said. "Best years of my life."

"Wow," Betsy said. "What's your secret?"

"Never go to bed angry," Tess said. "Always make your marriage merry with laughter and fun. Andy always made me laugh."

"Okay," Betsy said. "I'll take your advice to heart."

"You know when we were young, I asked Andy once what was the greatest thing known to man," Tess said.

"What did he say?" Betsy said.

"He said my vagina," Tess said. She giggled.

Betsy choked on her saliva. She smiled.

"I can believe it," Betsy said.

"I bet if he were alive today, he wouldn't say that," Tess said.

"Tess, I'd like to take your blood pressure," Betsy said.

"Okay," Tess said.

Betsy wrapped the cuff around Tess's arm, inserted the stethoscope earpieces, and positioned the metal disk over the brachial artery. She began squeezing the inflation bulb, watching the gauge rise in steady increments.

"Just relax your arm," Betsy said.

To Betsy's dismay, the bulb began squeezing on its own. Betsy dropped the bulb onto the bedspread out of terror. She watched as the aneroid manometer gauge needle climbed without assistance, ticking past dangerous numbers. Tess's face cringed with pain. She watched in horror as the bulb began to inflate and deflate faster and faster.

"You're hurting me," Tess said.

Crimson trickled from Tess's ears, then her nose, streaming upward against gravity into the IV line shooting back up into the saline bag. The saline bag reminded Betsy of a lava lamp when heated. The wax changes shape within the water, causing a mesmerizing cycle of slow-moving blobs that form like clouds and then sink, repeating the hypnotic motions. But although the blood in the saline bag didn't form blobs at first it did, however, act just as insoluble with the solution not mixing with it only instead of blobs, streaks of crimson made defined lines like strands of bleach blonde frosted hair intertwine with long wavy brunette. The streaks of blood joined to form a solid, floating mass. At first, it appeared to be a clot no larger than a thumbnail. But as she squinted, the contours sharpened, gaining definition until it was unequivocal—there. As Betsy inspected the saline bag further, she saw suspended within the colorless solution the unmistakable silhouette of a tiny, delicate life form suspended in the sterile liquid, a perfect miniature of a fully formed human being. The small, delicate fingers of the baby girl were curled into a fist; the tiny fingernails were almost invisible. Her face was peaceful, with her eyes sealed, a button nose, and soft, rosy cheeks. Her thumb rested against her lips as she slumbered. The plastic skin of the IV bag stretched tight with the weight of this miraculous creation, now twice its original size, on the verge of bursting with the life it held. Betsy found herself unable to look away. The baby's head bobbed in the fluid as if it were circulating. Betsy felt a rush of maternal grief; she wanted, desperately, to touch the cold plastic and draw it close.

From its side view, the infant spun at a snail's pace on its axis, drawn by invisible currents. As it orbited to face her, Betsy saw that the baby's skin had taken on the appearance of having sunburn. It had reddened from the saline solution. The color spread, starting as a faint blush at the fingertips and toes; it intensified to an angry red. Soon, the entire surface of the baby's skin had taken on the appearance of a raw, weeping burn.

The lids unsealed, revealing that there were no eyes. In their place, two perfect spheres radiated a red glow. A faint, high-pitched keening sound emerged from the bag; perhaps a child's cry for its mother. The noise could drive someone to madness, just as effectively as waterboarding. The old woman's lips moved in perfect synchrony with the infant's mouth, even though Tess's body lay limp, her eyes rolled back and white like eggshells. In that moment, the sound ceased, and Betsy felt a wave of relief wash over her.

"Hi Mommy, Mrs. McMillan said," came the words from Mrs. McMillan's mouth, but in the unmistakable voice of Betsy's son.

When Betsy looked back at Tess, the elderly woman's tired features had melted away. An eager young boy's persona, like that of her twelve-year-old son, smiled up at her, carefree and painless.

"Blake, is that you?" Betsy said, feeling uneasy talking to an old woman as she would her young son.

"You betcha, Mom." The childish temperament on the old woman's lips sent ice through Betsy's veins.

She felt, with mounting terror, that Mrs. McMillan—the vessel—had become her son's puppet.

"Let me get this blood pressure cuff off you, Blake," Betsy said, tugging at the Velcro.

"Aww, that's okay, Mom, Daddy said I need to lose weight if I want to play baseball," Blake's voice said.

Betsy pulled at the Velcro, but it wouldn't budge. The cuff tightened on its own.

Tess's blood seeped into the white bed linens.

"Look, Mommy—I'm losing weight!" The boyish voice giggled as Tess's body bled. The childish pride in the statement was almost more than Betsy could bear.

"Stop this," Betsy said, with tears streaming down her face, pleaded to whoever or whatever was causing this bizarre, unexplainable phenomenon. "Please stop."

Tess started coughing.

"Did you know blood weighs eight and a half pounds?" The voice continued eerily educational. "My biology teacher told us."

The coughing intensified, coming at shorter intervals, more forceful bursts.

"Daddy's gonna be so proud—eight whole pounds."

Tess began coughing without stopping. She hunched forward, clutching the bedsheet in her grip. The old woman's eyes watered, veins bulged along her temples, her mouth gaping open. The coughs tore through her, shaking her frail frame, her thin chest heaving with each desperate gasp.

"Mrs. McMillan, are you okay?" Betsy said, watching the woman's face turn scarlet. Something was blocking her airway. Acting on instinct, Betsy positioned herself behind Tess and performed the Heimlich maneuver. She looped her arms around the brittle ribcage, searched for the right spot, braced her legs, locked her fists, and drove upward and inward. After several thrusts, a hard piece of candy shot from the woman's mouth onto the bedsheet.

"Thanks, Mom! Close call," Blake's voice said.

Betsy couldn't force her eyes away from the candy, backing toward the door on unsteady legs.

"Where are you going? I wanted to practice my Morse code!" The voice called after her as she fled.

Once past the threshold, Betsy watched as the door closed.

"Betsy," Mrs. McMillan's voice—her normal voice—called from inside.

Betsy stared at the door for a moment, her hand trembling. The image of blood seeping into white sheets flashed in her mind. She couldn't abandon a patient and just let Mrs. McMillan bleed to death. She had to do something. She needed to take control of her thoughts and emotions.

"Betsy," Mrs. McMillan said again, this time with a concerned tone in the elderly woman's voice.

"Mrs. McMillan, is that you?" Betsy said, gapping the door just enough to peer through with one eye.

The room appeared normal—no blood, no grotesque swelling IV bag. Mrs. McMillan sat upright in bed, confusion wrinkling her brow.

"Are you alright, dear?" Mrs. McMillan said.

Betsy swallowed.

"Yes, fine."

"Are you finished taking my blood pressure?" Mrs. McMillan said. "I sure would like to get back to sleep."

Betsy noticed the cuff still wrapped around the woman's arm. Mrs. McMillan lifted her elbow just enough to draw attention to it.

"Oh, sorry," Betsy said, stepping fully into the room. "Yes, I'm finished."

She removed the cuff and placed it by the headboard.

"Thank you for keeping me safe," Mrs. McMillan said.

"Of course," Betsy said. "Just buzz if you need anything."

"Good night," Mrs. McMillan said.

"Sleep well," Betsy said, flicking off the light.

In the hallway, no more did the door click shut did Betsy noticed that something was off. She froze, with the hairs on her arms standing up. Thirty feet away, an empty wheelchair sat in the center of the corridor, unfolded and facing her. Her attention, that no one had bothered to collapse or push it against the wall, intensified her awareness that the chair wasn't there a moment before. As she stared, the chair inched toward her, its wheels turning without human hands. Betsy backed away, her eyes fixed on the approaching object. The wheelchair sped up. She turned and ran, the squeak of rubber wheels growing louder behind her. At the nurse's station, she vaulted onto the counter just as the wheelchair shot past, slamming into the wall-mounted water fountain. Metal shrieked against metal. A stack of clipboards scattered, some landing on the floor. Water sprayed from ruptured pipes while electrical sparks showered the floor. The wheelchair lay twisted on its side as overhead lights pulsed erratically. Betsy grabbed the fire extinguisher, dousing the sparks before they could spread, then twisted the water valve shut with trembling fingers. The water pressure dropped at once; the gushing fountain subsided to a trickle and then stopped.

CHAPTER 24

Jennifer lingered under the pattering stream of water, steam rising in a veiled curtain before her eyes. She was in the nurse's lounge, but not in comfort—more in defeat. She tried to focus only on the heat as it battered her shoulders, tried to forget the humiliation of the day. If she closed her eyes, she could almost imagine herself at home, in her own immaculate bathroom, washed in the honeyed glow of her makeup mirror, safe from petty spurts of cruelty. But when she opened them, she found Tammy shuffled in, arms loaded with a teetering pile of towels and clothing. She forced a smile while removing her skeleton earrings, which she set on the soap ledge.

"I hope you don't mind some granny panties," Tammy said, holding up a pair of full-sized peach briefs for Jennifer to see.

Jennifer tried to make well her friendly spirits by entertaining Tammy with a cringe-worthy expression as being the least likely choice for an undergarment, while keeping her wounded pride just beneath the surface.

"I stole them from Rose's room. I figured she's wouldn't need them anymore," Tammy said.

Jennifer mouthed a silent thank you. Tammy smiled in response.

"Maybe I'll give Rosslyn a sedative," Tammy said, with a sly wink.

That put a smile on Jennifer.

"I'll just set these here," Tammy said, placing the stack of clothes on the wooden bench.

Jennifer nodded.

"Well, okay then," Tammy said, "take as long as you need," then she left, shutting the door behind her.

Jennifer was alone once more.

Just as Tammy left, a tear or two escaped from Jennifer's right eye, onto her cheek like a skier leaping from the top of the hill onto the slippery, snow-covered slope. She wiped it away with the heel of her palm. The air was thick with moisture; the mirror above the sink had already filmed over with fog. She reached for the shutoff valve but hesitated. The temperature in the room had plummeted. She exhaled and saw her own breath, a billow of steam that hung in the air, refusing to dissipate, just as it does while inside the walk-in freezer. She raised her eyebrows in surprise. The water spray trickled to a stop, much like when she was gardening and kinked the hose to switch nozzles. She wrapped her arms around herself, as if she were protecting her bare breasts while cradling a bar of soap. The moment her right hand touched the shut-off valve, she sensed something was off. Her hand stuck to the cold metal handle. Her body craved heat, and she began to shiver. Beneath her feet, the water that had pooled hardened, small crystalline fractals etching themselves outward in a silent, mesmerizing bloom. As she attempted to step towards the hanging white towel, her feet felt glued to the tile floor. A wave of nausea washed over her, realizing that if she tried to free herself from the chilling grip, it would come at a painful cost. She watched the showerhead crusting over with frost as if watching a time-lapse video of its rapid formation. The frost spread like a shadow, turning everything it touched to white. It grew like fire taking over anything wet. When the frigid mist reached her feet, she could only watch helplessly in agony as fingers of fog crept up her thighs, causing her skin to feel the sting of frostbite. She fought back tears, fearing they might lead to blindness. The last of the water runoff streamed down her back, froze into ice formations that resembled veins branching out; clinging to her buttocks like tape. When she brushed the frozen droplets from her reddened skin, they clattered against the tile like hard candy. Her mind flashed with remembrances—childhood winters, the time she and her sister had snuck out to skate on a half-frozen pond, how their mother found out and scolded them telling them she prays they don't one day end up like popsicles in the morgue. Jennifer had laughed to the point of wetting herself. But now, the cold was not a game. It stung her skin, burned her lungs. She tried to move, but her feet had bonded to the tile, as if the frost was alive, intent on swallowing her whole. She needed to escape before she froze to death. She let out a scream, but the ice served as a barrier, and the thunderclap simultaneously drowned out her plea for help.

The frost spread in an impossible, accelerating tide; it snaked up her legs, over her knees, across her torso. Her teeth were chattering. A film of ice advanced across the mirror, obscuring the face that once peered back at her. She squinted and saw words trailing down the center of the mirror. The letters were eerily similar to the ones on Kate's windshield; the last words she read before losing consciousness.

"Trick or treat."

CHAPTER 25

Missy and Beth had just finished cleaning up Mr. Rosslyn Winters when they heard a loud crash up the hall. When they got to the nurses' station, they watched as Betsy sprayed a fire extinguisher at the collision site. Tammy approached, wearing a worried expression, as Betsy was turning off the valve on the damaged drinking fountain, stopping the leak.

"We heard a loud noise," Beth said.

"What happened?" Tammy said.

"I wouldn't begin to know how to explain it without sounding completely and utterly out of my mind," Betsy said, hands trembling as she rested the fire extinguisher against the counter.

Tammy gave her a flat look, arms crossed.

"Try me."

"Alright, according to science, if you can't see, touch, smell, hear, or taste something, it doesn't exist," Betsy said, emphasizing each word by ticking them off on her fingers.

"Our five senses," Beth said.

"Right," Tammy said.

"Well, this didn't happen," Betsy said, gesturing to the wheelchair tipped over on its side; one wheel still slowly spinning.

Missy chuckled.

"Have you been experimenting with the medicine?"

"So, am I to believe that you didn't shove this wheelchair into the drinking fountain?" Tammy said.

"Correct," Betsy said. "It chased me."

Beth and Tammy's eyes followed Betsy's gaze.

"Where's Jennifer?" Betsy said.

"Taking a shower," Missy said.

"A shower," Betsy said.

"Yeah," Missy said. "She slipped on Rosslyn's poop."

"He's now in diapers," Tammy said.

"Oh, gross," Betsy said.

"Yeah, it was pretty foul," Tammy said. "I told her to take as long as she needed. She's been in there for like twenty minutes, maybe more."

"Who wants pizza?" Missy said, entirely too cheerful for the moment. They all collapsed into their chairs.

"Who can eat after what I've just been through?" Betsy said.

"Especially after seeing what Jennifer had for lunch," Tammy said.

"Yeah, I seem to have lost my appetite as well," Beth said.

"Betsy, your hands are shaking," Tammy said. "Are you all right?"

Betsy took a deep breath and nodded.

The lights flickered overhead.

"Don't you think it's unsafe to take a shower during an electric storm? She could get electrocuted," Missy said.

"I should go check on her," Tammy said.

"Wait," Betsy said.

Tammy paused and looked at her.

"Be careful," Betsy said.

Tammy nodded and walked away.

CHAPTER 26

Tammy entered where she had last seen Jennifer showering not more than half an hour before—then very much alive and soapy. She heard the shower still running and noticed Jennifer's signature Charlie perfume stood on the sink countertop. It took seconds for Tammy's eyes to adjust and her mind to accept the shape she saw: not Jennifer standing, but Jennifer sprawled, nude, and supine on the tiles. Tammy made no sound at first. Her legs locked, her breath caught, chest fluttering as if she'd been sucker-punched. For a long moment, she only watched the water stream over Jennifer's bare, lacerated feet and hands, then she noticed something sickening: the skin at the bottom of Jennifer's feet and the tips of her fingers had torn, almost as if Jennifer had clawed at the tile in her final moments. The drain at the center of the shower room gurgled, overwhelmed by a mass, something white—something that, on closer inspection, seemed to be shreds of Jennifer's own skin.

Like a thief in the night, the ice and frost that crept in after Tammy's initial visit had vanished, leaving no trace behind.

From the nurses' station, Missy, Betsy, and Beth heard Tammy's scream. Betsy reacted in that instant, with Beth following her lead. Missy tossed her half-eaten slice of pizza into the delivery box and rushed to assist.

While Tammy stood in shock, gazing over Jennifer's naked body on the floor, Betsy, Beth and Missy approached with caution, breaths shallow, eyes wide and whites showing.

"Oh my gosh," Missy said, "She's been struck by lightning."

Tammy kneeled beside Jennifer's lifeless body, reaching for her carotid artery, hesitated, then touched two fingers to the hollow of Jennifer's throat, then recoiled.

"What's wrong?" Betsy said.

"She's cold," Tammy said.

"Well, that's how dead people feel," Missy said.

"I don't think so," Tammy said.

"What do you mean you don't think so?" Missy said, irritation creeping into her voice. "You don't think she's dead?"

"I mean, I don't think it was lightning," Tammy said.

"But her hands and feet are bloody," Missy said.

"That's a sign of electrocution, with the high voltage flowing to the path of least resistance," Betsy said.

"I'm surprised her pepperonis didn't get burned," Missy said.

"Excuse me, but did you just refer to Jennifer's areolas as pepperonis?" Tammy said.

"In a manner of speaking, yes," Missy said.

"Oh my gosh," Betsy said, "this can't be happening."

Again, Tammy felt Jennifer's pulse.

"She's as frozen as a popsicle," Tammy said.

"Shut off that water before the lightning kills us all," Missy said to Beth.

Beth tiptoed over, twisted the valve without resistance, reducing the steady stream to just a drip or two.

"I'll go grab the stretcher," Tammy said.

As she walked away, she overheard Missy said, "I wonder how many bodies you can stack before they topple over."

Beth and Betsy exchanged glances at Missy; neither of them said what they were thinking, which was probably for the best. Their expressions said it all.

CHAPTER 27

While Tammy, Missy, and Beth tended to Jennifer's body, Betsy was making her rounds, peeking in each room as she made her way down the hall. She expected to find all the residents sound in slumber despite the thunderclaps outside.

Some people sleep better during storms, she thought. So why is everyone awake?

What puzzled Betsy wasn't just that the residents were awake; it was that those who were awake were transfixed by the television. They all exhibited the same trance-like state she had observed in Tess McMillan. Except for Jed. When Betsy reached Jed's room, she found him sitting up in bed, engrossed in a book, with the television volume turned down low.

"Hi, Jed," Betsy said, stepping inside.

He looked up from the book and adjusted the reading glasses perched on his nose.

"Betsy," Jed said with a smile. "Come on in."

"I'm just making my rounds," Betsy said. "You need anything?"

"Couldn't sleep. Figured a little light reading might do the trick," Jed said, holding a book open and wearing reading glasses.

"What are you reading?" Betsy said.

"The Holy Bible," Jed said.

Betsy glanced at the book's spine and saw the gold letters: THE HOLY BIBLE.

"Interesting."

"Yes indeed," Jed said.

"What part are you reading?" Betsy said.

"Numbers, chapter twenty-two. The story of Balaam and his donkey."

"Balaam?" Betsy said. She had gone to church as a child, but couldn't remember all the stories to save her life.

"Yes indeed," Jed said, nodding once, as if to himself. "Balaam was a prophet. His donkey sees an angel that Balaam can't, so God makes the donkey speak. Tries to save his life."

"An animal spoke to a human?" Betsy said.

"Yes," Jed said.

"Sometimes I think animals are smarter than humans," Betsy said.

"When referring to those who claim the world is overpopulated, I couldn't agree more," Jed said. "Like the self-centered, godless folks who believe the deserts and beaches are running out of sand for making glass. The same people who believe that the all-knowing God, who knows every hair on your head would create a world too small for humans to inhabit."

"Do you read from chapter to chapter in order or do you skip around randomly, choosing a particular part that sparked your interest?" Betsy said.

"I've done both," Jed said. "I've read it all the way through, but now I mostly skip around."

"What are you using as a bookmark?" Betsy said.

She pulled it from the open book.

"It's 3D glasses," Jed said.

Betsy put the glasses on and smiled as she glanced around the room.

"Why are you using 3D glasses for…," Betsy said, but paused as her gaze landed on the television screen. Her smile faded, and her expression went blank.

"I used to own a 3D television back when my house was my home," Jed said. He noticed Betsy was quiet. "What's the matter?"

The 3D glasses filtered through the gray static on the television, revealing a message that was invisible to the naked eye: Trick or Treat.

A cold shiver ran up her arms. She blinked in rapid succession, her heart pounding in her chest. The message remained. Trick or treat. Unaware that Jed was watching her with curiosity, she pushed the glasses down to the bridge of her nose, peering over them at the same screen. The text was gone from the screen. She repeated this movement several times until Jed started to say something but cleared his throat instead. Realizing her actions were causing him concern, she returned to her usual relaxed demeanor, pretending everything was fine by letting Jed observe her as she closed her left eye and then opened it, repeating the process with her right eye, as if she was enjoying the experiment looking through the blue and red plastic lenses.

"Are you okay?" Jed said.

"Do you mind if I borrow these for a few minutes?" Betsy said.

Jed shrugged.

"Be my guest. Wasn't doing me much but holding my place. It's not like I'm getting a new 3D television installed anytime soon. A paper towel will mark my spot just as well."

She nodded, tucking the glasses into her pocket.

"Are you sure I can't bring you something?" Betsy said. "Missy brought in some chocolate cupcakes with an edible eyeball in the icing."

Jed's face lit up.

"Well, now that you mention it, that does sound like an irresistible treat."

"Alright then," Betsy said as she walked away, pondering Jed's choice of words: irresistible treat.

CHAPTER 28

"Something feels off," Betsy said as she approached the nurse's station counter.

"What do you mean?" Tammy said.

"Have you noticed how all the residents seem fixated on the television?" Betsy said.

"Maybe they can't sleep with all the thunder outside," Tammy said.

"I checked on Tess McMillan," Betsy said. "When I entered her room, she was in a trance-like state, staring at the television. She grabbed my arm as if she thought I meant to hurt her. Look."

Betsy showed the group the red mark on her arm.

"Was it dark?" Missy said.

"No, the light was on," Betsy said.

"The light was on but nobody was home?" Missy said.

"She acted like she didn't recognize me," Betsy said.

"Maybe she was just waiting for the reception to come back so she wouldn't miss any updates about the storm," Tammy said.

"Or maybe there's more to their madness," Betsy said.

She handed Tammy the pair of 3D glasses.

"These are 3D glasses," Tammy said.

"That's right," Betsy said. "I want you to put them on and look up at the static on the television screen."

Tammy hesitated for a moment but eventually slipped them on and gazed at the screen as Betsy continued speaking.

"Whoa," Tammy said. "That's freaky."

"Then when I tried to take her blood pressure…," Betsy said, struggling to contain her emotions.

"What?" Tammy said, lowering the glasses slightly down her nose to focus on Betsy.

"Did something happen? Did you see anything unusual? Perhaps something that seemed out of place so to speak?" Beth said.

"Yeah, how'd you know?" Betsy said.

"I think Jennifer saw something too," Beth said.

"What do you mean by something?" Tammy said, adjusting the glasses again for another look at the television while remaining engaged in the conversation.

"I'm not sure," Beth said. "I can't quite explain it."

"Intuition," Betsy said.

"Yeah, something like that," Beth said.

"Those are the same words that were written on Kate's windshield," Tammy said. "It's like steganography."

"And what is that?" Missy said.

"It's when someone hides a secret message in plain sight, and the receiver uses a key, or in this case, a colored filter, to reveal it," Tammy said.

"Like when we were kids and wrote notes in lemon juice. It was like invisible ink. But if you applied heat, the message would appear," Betsy said.

"But I don't see any residences wearing 3D glasses," Missy said.

"Right, but the subconscious mind can still pick it up," Tammy said. "It's known as subliminal perception."

"For instance," Betsy said. "Years ago, a single frame of popcorn would be inserted into a movie by the theaters. It passed by so quickly that the conscious mind didn't notice it, but the subconscious did, and theaters sold more popcorn as a result. That popcorn kernel was a subliminal message."

"There's something else," Beth said.

"What?" Betsy said.

"Cloreese told me there was no storm," Beth said.

"You're talking about the little girl," Betsy said.

Missy laughed.

"And you believed her?" Tammy said.

"I need to check something out first before I can answer that," Beth said.

"I looked for her. So, either she's a ghost or just a figment of your imagination," Betsy said.

Tammy removed the glasses and handed them to Missy. But when Missy raised them to her eyes, all she saw was static. There was no message.

Tammy said what she saw was the same words written on Kate's windshield, Beth thought.

"I don't see anything," Missy said. "You all are just playing a trick on me."

Beth considered for a moment the correlation between having fear and giving strength to the storm. It appears one feeds the other; keeping us captive and leaving us cut off from getting help, Beth thought. Missy was afraid of storms, which made her more likely to break down. The storm was gaining control over her.

"You see nothing but static?" Tammy said.

"May I have a look?" Beth said.

"Here," Missy said, tossing the cardboard glasses to her. "There's nothing to see."

Beth placed the glasses over her eyes, and the screen flickered to life with a different message.

I'M BACK.

MRS. BENNETT.

"What do you see, Beth?" Missy said.

Beth considered the question and thought about how best to answer it. If she claimed she saw nothing, the group would think she had come unhinged as Missy had become, but if she echoed what everyone else saw, she would be safe.

"The same as everyone else," Beth lied.

"If what you say is true, then why isn't anyone curious about who sent the message?" Missy said.

"Maybe it's being broadcast through the network, and tomorrow, whoever is the number one caller wins a prize," Tammy said.

"Or maybe you're all just making me the butt of your joke," Missy said. "Under the circumstances, with the freezer filling up with familiar bodies, I don't find it funny."

The call system light board, central monitor console from patient to nurse, lit up like a Christmas tree. All at once, all the rooms, except for a few, lit up with residents needing assistance from the nurses.

"I need something for pain," said room 114.

"I need an enema," said room 120.

"My joints hurt," said room 105.

"It burns when I pee," said room 118.

"I need ice," said room 102.

"I'm thirsty," said room 112.

"I lost my teeth, you need to check the laundry," said room 100

"I need some cream for my hemorrhoids," said room 116.

"I need a laxative," said room 107.

"I need some marijuana," Tammy said.

Beth, you're going to love the graveyard shift. There's absolutely no action, Beth thought. Missy's words echoed in her mind. Yeah, right. So far, tonight had been the exact opposite.

"I thought you all said nothing happens on the graveyard shift," Beth said.

"My legs are on fire," Mr. Rosslyn Winters from room 119 said.

"Now that's not typical," Missy said.

Mr. Winters didn't sound bossy this time; they could hear the fear in his voice. He was scared, pleading for mercy.

"Please help me," Mr. Winters said.

"I'll check it out, Tammy said.

"Good," Betsy said. "I'll take Beth with me to help calm these residents down."

"If you cover the East wing, I'll handle the West," Missy said.

"Deal," Betsy said. "Let's do this."

Betsy grabbed a cupcake for Jed while Beth clutched the 3D glasses.

CHAPTER 29

The scream shattered the hush of the night shift. Tammy hurried down the hallway toward the source of the noise. By the time she reached Rosslyn Winters' doorway, his panic had led to more pleading. His legs spasmed the way a lizard's tail does after you slice it off.

"Please make it stop; put it out," Rosslyn said.

"What seems to be the problem?" Tammy said.

"Can't you see," Rosslyn said, "my legs are on fire."

Tammy looked at his covered legs and then pulled back the blankets to reveal his bare skin. But there was no flame, no heat, no actual sign of an emergency beyond the terror on his face.

"There's no fire," Tammy said.

"He was sitting at the foot of my bed staring at me with those red eyes," Rosslyn said, crying, the words poured out like blood from a severed artery.

"Who was?" Tammy said.

"Help me, please help me." Rosslyn said, "Douse the fire. I'm burning."

Tammy scanned his legs but saw nothing out of the ordinary. Still, she could see it on his face. He believed he was having excruciating pain.

"My God, the pain. Stop the pain," Rosslyn said. "I don't want to die."

In a rush, Tammy dashed to the restroom, soaked a towel in cold water, wrung it out, and hurried back to him in an effort to calm him down.

If this doesn't work, I'll need to give him something for the pain, she thought.

When she returned, Rosslyn was motionless.

"Rosslyn, are you okay?" Tammy said.

He didn't respond.

Tammy checked his wrist and found no pulse. She examined his carotid artery. Nothing.

The hall outside was quiet again; the wailing had stopped.

Rosslyn was dead.

CHAPTER 30

A single knock, followed by three, and then two. That was Missy's signature way of announcing herself before entering a room.

"Missy, is that you?" Ethel Wallace said.

"It's me, Mrs. Wallace," Missy said.

"I didn't recognize you at first," Wallace said.

"I'm wearing a Halloween costume I made for tonight," Missy said.

"That must be it," Wallace said.

"Is the storm keeping you up?" Missy said. "Do you need something to help you relax?"

"I'm practically deaf without my hearing aid, but the lightning flashes at the window are annoying," Wallace said.

"Well, it's a good thing you're wearing your hearing aid otherwise you wouldn't be able to hear me," Missy said, speaking louder than the normal speaking level.

"Don't take this the wrong way, but I don't think you're grossly obese," Wallace said.

"Well, that's good to know," Missy said. "But how did my weight become the topic of the hour?"

"That's the way Jack put it," Wallace said, lying. "He mentioned you're the one carrying all the weight around here."

"Jack? As in the maintenance man Jack?" Missy said.

"One and the same," Wallace said.

"Jack said I was grossly obese? Or was he implying I do more work than the others?" Missy said.

"The former," Wallace said, continued her deception.

"That's so mean," Missy said.

"Don't blame me; I'm just relaying what Jack told me," Wallace said, trying to provoke Missy.

"Uh-huh, uh-huh," Missy said.

Using her right index finger and thumb, she wiped the corners of her mouth in a sign of irritation. Her frustration was growing, but she was trying to keep it hidden. Her cheeks were flushing red.

"I'm on your side; I thought you'd want to know," Wallace said.

"So, when did you talk to Jack?" Missy said.

"I might have dozed off a bit, but it was a few hours ago. He was heading to fix some lights in another room," Wallace said.

"Uh-huh," Missy said.

"He said you looked like you'd gained a ton of weight. He referred to you as thunder thighs," Wallace said.

"Oh, really?" Missy said, feeling even more perturbed.

"Yes, he said you brought in some pizza and were gorging yourself with it, like you were shoving a whole piece in your mouth, swallowing after hardly chewing it thoroughly," Wallace said.

"Go on," Missy said.

"He said if he ate that way he'd have constipation for a week," Wallace said. "He said he asked for a piece, and you snapped at him with your teeth like some ferocious dog."

"What else did Jacky boy say?" Missy said.

Ethel noticed she was riling Missy up.

"I shouldn't say anymore," Wallace said. "I've upset you, haven't I?"

"No, no, no, no, no, no, no. I'm fine," Missy said, lying. "Is there more?"

"Well, he did say that Betsy looked very nice in her costume tonight. He thought she seemed to have lost a few unwanted pounds, and now her outfit fits her perfectly. He thinks she jogs or exercises," Wallace said.

"No, that's Tammy," Missy said, as a matter of fact. "She jogs with her Labrador Retriever. Betsy is more of a couch potato."

"Oh, my misunderstanding," Wallace said. "He and Betsy bump into each other quite often, and I don't mean by chance, if you catch my drift."

"She's married," Missy said.

"So was Kate," Wallace said.

"Was?" Missy said.

"What?" Wallace said.

"You said was," Missy said. "What made you say was?"

Missy knew that Mrs. Wallace had no way of knowing Kate was dead.

"Isn't she divorced?" Wallace said.

"No, that's Tammy," Missy said.

"Oh, my bad," Wallace said.

"Sounds like Jacky had a lot to say," Missy said.

"He's such a nice boy, that Jack," Wallace said. "But I must admit, I don't agree with his opinion of your costume."

"My costume? What about my costume?" Missy said, recalling how she had attempted to clean Jack's blood off her outfit using cold water in the restroom earlier.

"He said it was stupid and immature," Wallace said. "Though he gave you one compliment."

"Oh yeah," Missy said, feeling the urgency to be praised.

"He said you definitely had the body for that costume," Wallace said.

"That's a compliment?" Missy said.

"I hate to be the one to break the bad news," Wallace said.

"Bad news?" Missy said. "Nonsense. I'm the one who has the bad news."

"I'm all ears," Wallace said.

"Jack lost some weight," Missy said.

"He looked…" Wallace said, but Missy interrupted her.

"Actually, since you last saw him, he's lost a considerable amount of weight," Missy said with a sarcastic grin.

"What are you saying?" Wallace said.

"Put this way, if he were wearing a costume, it would portray the scarecrow with its insides ripped out by flying monkeys," Missy said.

"Are you saying Jack is… is…" Wallace said.

"Dead," Missy said.

"What happened to him?" Wallace said.

"Does it really matter?" Missy said. "Dead is dead. So, he won't be making any more rude comments about my body any longer, and you won't be bothered with Mr. Perfect anymore. He's as dead as Goliath," Missy said with a fake smile.

"That's awful," Wallace said.

"Would you like to see him? We've got him lying in the walk-in freezer," Missy said.

"Oh, good heaven no," Wallace said.

"Well, okay then," Missy said with a hint of sarcasm. "If you change your mind, just give me a buzz at the nurse's station. I don't mind a bit."

With her mouth open in shock, Ethel watched Missy turn and walk away.

Missy paused for a second.

"Oh, and by the way," Missy said.

"Yes," Wallace said.

"I can't guarantee that Jack's bloody carcass lying in the freezer won't affect the taste of the food. My best advice to you is that when dinnertime rolls around, don't go with the fish. Toodles, Mrs. Wallace," Missy said before exiting the room.

CHAPTER 31

Betsy stepped into Jed's room, with Beth trailing behind her.

"Here's one chocolate cupcake, complete with an edible eyeball in the icing, just like I promised," Betsy said.

Jed remained motionless, fixated on the static-filled television screen.

"Jed, are you okay?" Betsy said.

Beth looked at the television.

"Don't look at the television," Betsy said to Beth.

Beth looked away.

Betsy yanked the electric cord from the wall, cutting off the screen's light.

"Jed, it's Betsy," she said.

Betsy shook Jed's shoulder. Jed's eyes came alive, shifting his focus to Betsy.

"Hi, Betsy," Jed said. "Sorry, I must've dozed off."

"I brought you a little something," Betsy said. She revealed a cupcake.

"Why thank you," Jed said. "It looks delicious."

He took a bite just as the T.V. flickered back on. Betsy noticed Beth staring at the unplugged cord.

"I think I got this," Beth said.

Beth handed the 3D glasses back to Jed.

"Thank you, Beth," Jed said.

"You two know each other?" Betsy said.

"I ran into him in the hallway earlier," Beth said.

Jed continued to chew the cupcake.

"We'll just tuck your cardboard glasses back into your Bible," Betsy said.

Beth positioned a chair under the television. Betsy shielded Jed's view with his book while Beth climbed onto the chair and yanked the television off the wall, carrying it into the hallway.

Betsy could hear the screen crunch as Beth dropped it onto the floor.

Jed stopped, having just wiped chocolate from his mouth, and realized that his television was missing.

"What happened to the T.V.?" Jed said.

"Beth tried to fix it, but she's not the best at repairs, so we'll need to get you a new one tomorrow," Betsy said.

"I'd prefer reading anyway," Jed said.

"They always say the book is better than the movie," Betsy said, pouring him a glass of water.

"I think I was dreaming," Jed said.

"But your eyes were open," Beth said, as she returned.

"What did you dream about?" Betsy said.

"That everyone was dead," Jed said. "The day shift staff arrived with the police shortly after. Someone walked right through me as I stood in the middle of the hallway. I felt like I was thirty again. They found everyone dead except for John Doe. He was never alive. Those eyes of his, coming from the depths of hell, glared at me like a prowler. I wasn't afraid. In my mind, I rebuked him."

"What does he want?" Betsy said.

"What does all evil want? Your soul, that's what," he said. "That's the treat; the sweet taste of victory. For every soul the devil claims, that's one more sorrowful spirit kept locked away, like a killer keeps a trophy or souvenir. It doesn't matter what happens to the body, not in that dream or in this place. It's the soul that gets counted. It's the only thing that matters, when you get right down to it."

"Just as a hunter will hang a deer's head and antlers on the wall," Betsy said.

"Misery loves company," Beth said.

"That's right, bull's-eye, you hit the mark," Jed said.

Beth remembered a time driving her cherry-red 1965 Mustang convertible, the wind whipping through her hair as she bopped along in the driver's seat to Jackie Wilson's "My Love Is Lifting Me Higher," which blasted from the speakers with an electrifying energy. Her ponytail swayed in perfect synchrony with the beat. She was high on energy. As she cruised along the sun-drenched road, she spotted a Chevrolet Corvair stranded on the side of the road. Her sunglasses slid down to rest on the bridge of her nose as she peered over the frames at Jed. A cloud of steam enveloped him while standing at the front of his car with the hood propped up, and he looked frustrated, as if he could use a miracle. Beth pulled over and offered him a ride, since they were going to the same place.

"Well, we'll let you get back to your reading," Betsy said.

"I'm going to catch some shuteye," Jed said.

"If you need anything else, just give us a buzz," Beth said, waiting by the door.

Betsy exited the room, with Beth tailing.

CHAPTER 32

Tammy entered Rosslyn Winters's room once again, this time with a stretcher. Each time she did so, her arms felt more strained, not just from the weight but from the awkwardness of maneuvering it and the prolonged effort required to transport each body to the walk-in freezer. This makes the fifth time tonight she has had to wrestle with this awkward thing. The stench of old sweat clung to the armpits of her clothes like a second skin, from having to carry the stretcher over and over throughout the night. The soft shuffling of her shoes on the floor broke the silence in the room. She leaned the stretcher against the bed, just missing her right foot. She glanced down, hoping she hadn't scuffed up her shoe, only to discover a dark blotch of blood on the tip of one. With a frown, she stooped to wipe it off. When she straightened up, her heart skipped a beat. Rosslyn was staring at her with a chilling, sinister grin, his vacant eyes rolled back to reveal only the whites, locked onto her with an unsettling intensity. Tammy stumbled backward, almost tripping over her own unsteady feet. She stood frozen, her mind swirling in disbelief as shock coursed through her. He was dead, yet he was staring—he shouldn't have been able to do so.

"Hell is real," Rosslyn said. "You'll be here too, real soon."

Then, as if someone knocked him out, Rosslyn was gone.

In a frantic rush, she lunged for the corner of the sheet, flinging it over his head like a fisherman casting a net into the sea, desperate to shield herself from his nightmarish face. She yanked the sheet up and over his head so hard she came close to pulling it off the far side of the bed.

From under the sheet, a sound broke the stillness—a low, bubbling giggle that chilled her to the bone.

"Trick or treat, smell my old feet, give me some fresh flesh to eat," Rosslyn's corpse said.

CHAPTER 33

Betsy checked in on Mrs. Grace Gallows, who appeared to be resting well. When Betsy touched her arm, Mrs. Gallows felt clammy.

"Mrs. Gallows, I'm going to take a glucose test," Betsy said.

Beth observed as Betsy positioned the spring-loaded needle against Mrs. Gallows' index finger and pressed the trigger, releasing the sharp point into her skin. The small puncture yielded enough blood for the test.

Beth watched as the blood traveled up the test strip, which reminded her of sperm racing towards an egg, though she'd never admit to such girlish thoughts.

"You'll become familiar with the diabetics and learn how often to check for high sugar levels," Betsy said.

Beth listened with interest as someone who's eager to learn.

"Just as I suspected," Betsy said.

"What's the reading?" Beth said.

"631," Betsy said.

"Wow," Beth said, recalling from her Aunt Ripley, who was diabetic, that this reading was quite high.

"Do you know where we moved the insulin?" Betsy said.

"No," Beth said.

"That's right, Jennifer was giving you the tour when we moved it from the nurse's station to the walk-in refrigerator in the kitchen," Betsy said.

"Where we placed Jennifer," Beth said.

"Do you think you can find it?" Betsy said.

"Of course," Beth said.

"Good. Draw me one unit of Humalog, stat," Betsy said.

Beth left the room as Tammy entered.

"Do you think you can help me?" Tammy said.

"She needs an insulin shot," Betsy said. "I'm waiting for Beth to return."

"Okay," Tammy said.

"What's going on?" Betsy said.

"Rosslyn Winters just died," Tammy said.

"What? Jeez-o-Pete," Betsy said. "We have some explaining to do in the morning."

Tammy nodded.

"You're busy. I'll see if I can track down Missy," Tammy said.

"If you can't find her, Rosslyn can wait," Betsy said. "Once I give this shot, Beth and I will help you."

"Okay," Tammy said. "If you don't hear back from me, you'll know I've found Missy."

"Okay," Betsy said.

Tammy left the room.

CHAPTER 34

Tammy spotted Missy wandering the hallway.

"Missy," Tammy said.

"Yes," Missy said.

"Could you help me with Rosslyn Winters?" Tammy said.

"Don't tell me you need help changing his diaper?" Missy said.

"I'm afraid not," Tammy said. "He died a few minutes ago, and I need help carrying him to the freezer."

"Well, of course he's dead," Missy said. "Why wouldn't he be dead? Everyone else is dying; why not him?"

Tammy looked confused.

"Are you okay?" Tammy said.

"Why does everyone keep asking me that tonight?" Missy said. "I mean, if the Health Department pays us a visit, they'll think we're serving Soylent Green. Do you not get that?"

"What is Soylent Green?" Tammy said.

"Just forget it," Missy said.

"Look, never mind," Tammy said. "I can get Beth and Betsy to help."

"Don't get your panties in a wad," Missy said. "I'll help you carry another corpse to the makeshift morgue."

CHAPTER 35

While inside the kitchen's walk-in refrigerator, Beth had been hoping to find Cloreese to help her. She remembered much of her studies in nursing school; she struggled with the clinical aspects and had eventually dropped out because of a lack of interest, opting to switch her major to English with a minor in education instead. She was holding an empty syringe in her right hand when she heard Jennifer's voice calling out to her.

"Beth, let me out," the voice said, pleaded. "I'm freezing in here."

Beth closed the refrigerator door and moved to the walk-in freezer, where Jennifer's frozen body lay behind the door. With her heart racing, she reached for the handle.

"Jennifer, is that you?" Beth said.

She wasn't certain if the voice was in her head or coming from outside. She pulled the handle, allowing time to mingle with molasses, while inching the freezer door open. A cloud of fog poured out, and for a moment, obscured her view inside. Once the mist cleared, she searched for any sign of movement among the frozen figures. Jennifer's body remained where she and Tammy had left it. Beth shut the door, and it latched. Turning around, she saw Betsy rushing toward her in a state of frantic.

"Did you get it?" Betsy said.

Beth almost stabbed Betsy with the syringe.

"Hey watch it," Betsy said, forcing Beth's arm down to bring the syringe to a safe distance at her side.

"Sorry, you scared me," Beth said, extending the syringe toward Betsy. "Here."

Betsy raised an eyebrow.

"The insulin isn't in the freezer," Betsy said. "I told you it was in the walk-in refrigerator."

"Sorry," Beth said.

Betsy entered the refrigerator and drew one unit of Humalog into the syringe before leaving in a hurry, not waiting for Beth to follow.

Meanwhile, Tammy and Missy were carrying Mr. Winters into the kitchen when they spotted Betsy jogging down the hall toward Mrs. Gallows' room.

In the kitchen, Missy caught Beth coming out of the freezer, holding Jennifer's phone.

"What do you think you're doing?" Missy said.

"I thought I heard something," Beth said.

"Was it coming from Jennifer's phone?" Missy said, noticing what was in Beth's left hand.

"What?" Beth said, following Missy's gaze. "Yeah, I suppose it could have."

"You know, the phone you were interested in earlier," Missy said.

"I assumed it would get ruined in there," Beth said.

"The cold could drain the battery," Tammy said.

"And if there's something on this that could help the police in their investigation and clear any suspicions of any foul play," Beth said.

"Yeah, like a picture or something," Tammy said.

"You didn't know about the battery?" Beth said, directing the question to Missy.

"Of course I know that," Missy said. "What do you think, I'm stupid?"

"What were you accusing me of?" Beth said. "Stealing Jennifer's phone?" With Tammy backing her up, Beth felt empowered to confront Missy.

"I most certainly was not," Missy said.

"Apologize," Beth said.

"I will not," Missy said.

"Apologize," Beth said again.

"No," Missy said. "Not even if you held a blade to my throat."

Missy set her end of the stretcher on the stainless-steel table and walked out of the kitchen.

Beth assisted Tammy in positioning Rosslyn's body with the others.

Once Beth stepped away from the freezer and closed the door behind her, Tammy turned to her.

"May I see the phone?" Tammy said.

Beth handed it over.

"What you said to Missy about wanting to save Jennifer's phone from being ruined," Tammy said.

"Yes," Beth said.

"Was that true or was there another reason?" Tammy said.

"Betsy mentioned that all the residents were staring at the televisions as if hypnotized," Beth said. "I thought if I took some photographs of the static on the screen…"

"The camera filter would protect you from harm?" Tammy said.

"Yes, of course," Beth said, not being very tech-savvy but agreed with Tammy's line of thought. It sounded reasonable to her, so she nodded.

"Good thinking," Tammy said. "Let's try it out."

"At the very least, we might provide some evidence for the police to support our claims of innocence," Beth said.

"You make a good point," Tammy said.

"I mean, I wouldn't believe me if I heard this crazy story about what happened tonight," Beth said.

"Me neither," Tammy said. "Well, let's try your theory out."

Beth hesitated.

"Wait. How'd you know I wasn't stealing it?" Beth said.

"Do you know Jennifer's password?" Tammy said.

"Well, no," Beth said.

"Neither do I," Tammy said with a smile. "Good thing we don't need one in this case."

"Why do you say that?" Beth said.

"This phone is set up to accept the owner's thumbprint for access," Tammy said.

"I'm clearly behind the times," Beth said, thinking of how true that statement was.

"You obviously didn't know that," Tammy said. "Once I gain access to her settings, I can disable the security feature, allowing me to access her phone anytime without needing her thumb."

Tammy took the phone into the freezer and used Jennifer's cold, lifeless thumb to unlock its settings. The screen lit up.

"Got it. Let's go," Tammy said.

CHAPTER 36

Betsy lifted Mrs. Gallows' gown and inserted the needle into her abdomen to administer the medication. After a moment, she checked the glucose levels again. Just then, Beth and Tammy walked into the room.

"Where have you been," Betsy said to Beth.

"She helped me with Rosslyn," Tammy said.

"Where was Missy?" Betsy said.

"She's like, scattered brain," Tammy said. "She helped me move Rosslyn to the kitchen, then accused Beth of stealing Jennifer's phone, and then just left in a fit of rage."

"I'm going to check Grace again in a second," Betsy said.

"I have Jennifer's phone," Tammy said.

"We thought we could take some pictures of the static on the screen as evidence in case the police don't believe us," Beth said.

"Good idea," Betsy said. "It appears the only eyes that aren't fixed on the television screen belong to those who are reading, heavily medicated, or have their faces covered, including a few who are praying."

Tammy aimed the camera at the television and snapped a few photos. Beth and Betsy crowded around Jennifer's phone as Tammy scrolled through the images. The television screen showed nothing but static in all three shots. Tammy swiped left until she reached the fourth recent photo, which was a group picture of the nurses at the nurse's station—the same one Kate had taken with Missy's phone. She went back to examine the static again.

"Wait," Betsy said. "Go back."

Tammy returned to the group photo.

"How did Jennifer get that picture?" Beth said.

"Missy must've sent it to her," Betsy said.

What was even more puzzling was that Kate appeared in the first picture but was absent from the second.

"Wait, this doesn't make any sense," Tammy said. "Look, Kate is in the picture. She was the one who took it."

"So who took the first picture?" Beth said.

Betsy and Tammy exchanged glances with Beth, unable to solve the mystery. They were all baffled and speechless.

Tammy moved on to the next photo. Jennifer was present in the second picture but missing from the third.

"Where's Jennifer in this one?" Betsy said.

Then Beth noticed Tammy staring at the fourth picture.

"What's wrong?" Beth said.

"Do you see me in the fourth picture?" Tammy said.

"Oh," Beth said. "What's that mean?"

"I must be next," Tammy said, looking up at Beth and Betsy.

CHAPTER 37

As Betsy made her way back to the nurse's station, she noticed Stella still sitting in her wheelchair.

"We need to get you into bed," Betsy said.

Stella stared at her with opaque corneas.

"It's a free country, isn't it?" Stella said. "I can go to bed whenever I want to."

"Come now, Stella," Tammy said. "You need your rest."

With Tammy on one side of Stella and Betsy and Beth on the other, they hoisted Stella, who felt like dead weight, toward the bed. They settled her in the center. Stella reached up and grabbed the flesh beneath Beth's forearm, squeezing with such force that she was gritting her false teeth. Beth screamed in pain, releasing her grip on Stella. Reacting out of instinct, she slapped Stella across the face; Stella dropped onto the bed hard. While Stella comforted her cheek with her left hand, Beth examined her arm where Stella's nails had broken the skin. Blood oozed from the cut. Tammy's eyes widened in shock. Stella chuckled.

"Someone's put on their big girl panties," Stella said. "Let's see how you manage to pry the wedgie out of your crack when I let the doctor know tomorrow."

"Maybe I should file an incident report for your abuse of a healthcare worker and get you transferred to a psych ward at Bellview," Beth said, with much conviction.

"Bellview," Stella said. "Why, that place shut down over ten years ago."

"Yeah, but I'm told that secret experiments are still being conducted there and their preferred choice are involuntary crazies, like yourself, to use as guinea pigs for their deadly vaccines," Beth said.

"Everyone knows they use foster children for experiments. Even when they refuse to participate, they're forced into taking drugs that have failed clinical trials," Stella said. "I even read somewhere that someone found a mass grave at a cemetery in Hawthorne, New York, where they dumped kids who died from those experiments into a hole just like the Jews in the Holocaust. They're expendable because they have no parents; it's easy to cover it up."

"Just like you," Beth said. "You're expendable, with no living parents, and you'd be so easy to cover up."

Stella's expression hardened, lips retreated, silence followed.

Beth stepped out into the hallway, leaning against the wall, tears streaming down her face. Tammy tried to comfort her.

"Don't let that ole' witch bother you," Tammy said. "I'll back up your story."

"I'm not crying over Stella," Beth said.

"Then what's wrong?" Tammy said.

"Mrs. Carmichael in room 117 has just died," Beth said.

"How do you know that?" Betsy said.

"Cloreese, the little girl, prophesied that when I smack a resident tonight, Mrs. Carmichael will have passed," Beth said.

"Well, let's go check on her," Tammy said.

CHAPTER 38

Missy was leaving Oscar Little's room when she spotted Betsy entering the men's restroom.

Why would Betsy be going in there? Missy thought.

She pressed her ear against the door and overheard Betsy speaking with Jack.

"I figured I'd find you here," Betsy's voice said.

"Where else would I be? After all this is the restroom, so I come here to rest," Jack's voice said.

They both laughed.

This can't be real, Missy thought. Jack is dead.

Missy heard them sucking each other's lips.

"What took you so long," Jack's voice said.

"I had to make sure Miss Thunder-Thighs didn't spot me," Betsy's voice said.

"What will you do if Missy finds out about us?" Jack's voice said.

"She's so stupid," Betsy's voice said. "I hope she cries herself to sleep."

Fueled by anger, Missy barged into the restroom, hoping to confront Betsy and whoever she was with, but the space was empty. Graffiti on the wall caught her attention. Inside a heart drawing were the words:

JACK & BETSY FOREVER, written elegantly.

A few inches away, jagged letters proclaimed: THUNDER THIGHS EATS SLOP LIKE ALL PIGS DO, scratched with a vengeful intensity.

Missy felt her cheeks flush as if someone had slapped her, her anger rising.

"Missy," said Jack's reflection, called from the mirror.

It's Jack, she realized, staring back at her.

"I thought you were dead," Missy said.

She started to turn and face him.

"Don't," Jack's voice said, as if he'd read her mind.

"Don't what?" Missy said, returned her gaze to face the mirror.

"Don't turn around," the reflection said.

"But Jack, I want to see you," Missy said.

"You see me," Jack's reflection said.

"Yeah, but it's not the same," Missy said, holding her position in front of the mirrors as Jack demanded.

"What's troubling you?" Jack's reflection said.

"The words on the wall hurt," Missy said.

"Where?" Jack said.

Looking back, she found the graffiti had vanished.

"Jack, do you think I'm heavy? Do you think my thighs are big?"

"What do you think?" Jack's reflection said.

"I think Betsy is smaller than I am, and it's not fair," Missy said.

"You sound weak and pathetic," Jack's reflection said. "Betsy is loyal. A man is at his best when treated like a king. No two seats can rule the throne. One king must leave or face death in a duel; defeat by a fight to the finish."

"I want to be your queen," Missy said.

"Are you stronger than she?" Jack's reflection said.

"Of course I am," Missy said.

"Then prove it," Jack's reflection said.

"But how?" Missy said.

"Make her weak, and you shall gain strength. Show me you are more loyal to me than she is, and you will earn my favor," Jack's reflection said.

"Make her weak?" Missy said.

"Yes," Jack's reflection said. "Now look into my eyes."

Missy stared at the center mirror, where Jack's eyes glowed red. The restroom door swung open, but no one entered or left. Her trance broke when the sound of the door shutting. Jack's reflection was gone. Water ran from the central faucet. She cupped her hands and splashed water on her face, streaking her mascara down her cheeks. Looking into the mirror, she said, "Betsy won't even see it coming."

CHAPTER 39

Betsy, Beth and Tammy checked in on Mrs. Carmichael in room 117. They found Mrs. Carmichael in bed; hands folded atop her Afghan. Her smile reassured the three of them that she had passed away peacefully. Betsy leaned over, tucking a stray wisp of silver hair back behind Martha's ear.

"Goodbye, Martha," Betsy said in a whisper, while placing her thumb and index finger on Martha's eyelids, closing her blank gaze forever.

"She looks so peaceful," Beth said. However, it wasn't Beth's voice that spoke; it was Betsy's.

Tammy and Betsy exchanged worried glances at Beth.

"Why do you sound like Betsy?" Tammy said to Beth, but her words came out in Beth's voice as if Beth were speaking through her.

"This is too weird," Betsy said, only for Tammy's voice to emerge from her lips. She flicked her tongue out, as if to test whether her mouth still belonged to her.

Tammy's forearms prickled with gooseflesh.

Mrs. Carmichael's landline phone rang.

All three shot a look toward the phone, hearts hummingbird-quick.

Beth reached for the handset.

"Don't," Betsy said to Beth. "Don't pick that up."

Beth withdrew her hand and looked back at Betsy.

"Listen," Tammy said.

"It sounds like every phone is ringing simultaneously," Beth said.

"So, what's next?" Tammy said, still speaking in Beth's voice. "Are all the old women going to start getting their periods again, and the older men having wet dreams?"

"It seems this little girl you keep mentioning knows things," Betsy said, using Tammy's voice. "Maybe she can help us."

"Her name is Cloreese," Beth said, channeling Betsy's voice, as though a ventriloquist had planted it there.

At that instant, every phone fell silent.

"That was freaky," Betsy said, her own voice returned.

"We need to take care of Mrs. Carmichael and pray for the eye of the storm to give us some temporary relief," Tammy said, with her own voice returned to normal as well.

"I'll second that," Betsy said. "I need to calm my nerves."

"I need to use the restroom," Beth said. "Do you mind…?"

"Go ahead," Betsy said. "Tammy and I can manage here."

"Are you sure?" Beth said.

"Go," Tammy said. She looked at Betsy. "I'll grab the stretcher."

Beth went toward the restroom while Tammy went for the stretcher.

CHAPTER 40

An alarm sounding in the adjacent room set Missy's feet into action. She rushed into Mrs. Julia Shadwack's room, where the patient was coding. Shaking Julia, she realized she was unconscious and without another single thought began resuscitation efforts through CPR. She positioned the heel of her left hand over her right, interlocking her fingers, and started compressing her chest thirty times. Missy counted aloud, a warped metronome: "One, two, three—." Then, she stopped, tilted her chin, pinched her nose, sealed Julia's mouth with her own, and gave two rescue breaths. Julia's lips were dry and sunken. Still, Missy delivered two breaths, felt the mushy resistance, the lack of spring, but she kept going. Three more cycles, until her arms were trembling, until her own breathing was laboring.

Why isn't anyone helping me? Do they not hear the alarm? She thought.

In her mind, Missy pictured Betsy with her feet propped up on the desk, eating her pizza, and laughing with Tammy and Beth while she struggled with trying to save this patient's life. Her frustration intensified with each compression.

"Don't you die," she said, sounding out of breath. Missy could feel the fractured rib beneath her palm.

After several cycles of chest compressions and breaths, she reached for the crash cart, yanked open the top drawer, and fumbled with the defibrillator pads. Her hands were slick and trembling, and when she finally got the pads in place, she remembered, too late, that Julia had a DNR band. It was blue, and it caught the light as she tore open the woman's gown, exposing the pale, slack skin of her chest. The band indicated a do not resuscitate order, yet the need to save this woman's life meant more to her than any protocol she was supposed to follow. What if Julia were standing outside her body right now, screaming for another chance with words as transparent as her body? Would by following a protocol that lacked sympathy haunt me until death? She thought. The thought of Beth's story crept into her mind—a man named Smith Wigglesworth, who she said had raised fourteen people from the dead without the help of any medical devices. Did he get into trouble? Her mind flickered to Pinky, her beloved pet pig, a bittersweet memory of innocence lost when her father had made the heart-wrenching decision to slaughter him. She reasoned with herself. Why couldn't it be Ethel Wallace lying here instead of this nice lady, she thought.

The machine whined, then emitted a green light, ready with the defibrillator primed for use. Missy positioned the paddles against Julia's bare, vulnerable chest, right above the heart, and hesitated. Her thumb hovered over the discharge button, trembling with uncertainty. She closed her eyes. The reflection of Jack in the bathroom mirror flashed in her mind. Before she could say rocking Robin, the paddles activated. Was it an involuntary movement? A twitch? Did Jack push her thumb? She'd triggered the shock button, sending 151.1 joules of energy surging through Julia's body. The body arched and fell, like a marionette, but the line on the monitor stayed flat. Julia's body gave nothing back. Missy reset the paddles and tried again. This time, the shocks continued to deliver over and over without needing to recharge; there were no pauses in the cycle. Despite her firm grip on the paddles, she felt powerless as Julia's body convulsed. The paddles continued to administer shocks until Julia was dead.

Missy was alone. She was always alone.

Overcome with rage, Missy screamed in fury, pressed the paddles to her own temples, and pulled the trigger, sending a shock wave through her brain. There was a brief static pop, then a brightness behind her eyelids—a flash, like the magnesium on a camera.

Would it be enough to erase the memory of being a failure, the humiliation?

She collapsed to the floor, and a stream of urine pooled between her calves.

CHAPTER 41

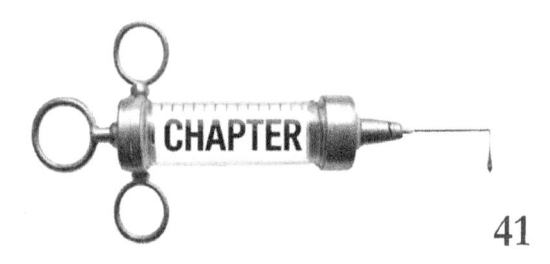

Beth stood before the door of room 115, where a makeshift danger sign crafted from taped-together pieces of fax paper hung across the entryway, its bold letters spelling out a clear warning for any curious onlookers.

Behind this door was Kate's car stuck in the wall, she thought.

When she first encountered the incident, the scene was gruesome with Jack's body almost severed in half, blood splattered everywhere, especially on Missy. Most of her attention centered on the windshield, where the words "Trick or Treat" were still visible through the condensation. The driver's side headlight was blinding, making it hard for anyone peering through the damaged wall from inside the building to see outside, especially with steam from the radiator fogging the area. She recalled the sound of water striking the part of Kate's car that jutted out, its impact louder than the water trickling in through the wreckage. Beth's mind associated the sound of water with rain and rain with a storm; however, after Cloreese mentioned that there was no storm, she remembered a news report from 1966 showing a distracted driver crashing into a fire hydrant in front of a burning school, nearly colliding with a student and a faculty member. The water had shot up fifty to sixty feet into the air. If Kate's car had knocked over a fire hydrant, the resulting spray could easily have been mistaken for rain, since the hearing sense seems more sensitive than sight at night because of the lack of visual references in the dark. This notion lingered in Beth's mind, but she questioned whether anyone else at the nurse's station watching the same broadcast had drawn similar conclusions or if they even noticed it at all.

Beth peeled away the paper barrier and stepped into the room where Kate's vehicle ended Jack's life, compelled to uncover the truth.

"The truth will set you free," she thought.

Inside, Beth switched on the lights. The room looked as it had before, with a bloodstain on the floor marking Jack's body. Whether the nursing home would suffer a drop in water pressure if the fire hydrant were to be damaged; after all, Jennifer could still take a shower. She concluded there must be a backup system, perhaps even regulations requiring nursing homes to have certain protocols in place to ensure residents had access to sufficient water pressure and clean drinking water if the city supply were to be compromised.

A secondary water system must exist; she considered.

As the door closed, the lights flickered out for a moment before blinking back on. The room had changed. Instead of the linoleum tiles she came to know in the nursing home, it now resembled her classroom from 1966. She noticed light streaming through the gaps around Kate's car and the existing wall. Looking outside, she saw it was daytime and spotted herself standing on the street, gazing up at the second-story window.

This building is only one story; how can this be? She thought.

Beth recalled that moment when the school was on fire, and she stood on the sidewalk gazing up at the second-story window. She was looking at a little girl calling for help. Now the roles have switched. Beth now found herself occupying the place at the window where the frightened little girl in 1966 was calling for help. It was as if now she was the little girl, yet she saw herself as an adult, standing alongside her students along the street with a sympathetic expression.

"Help me!" Beth called out to her adult self-standing below, but her voice came out high-pitched, childlike. When she looked down at her hands, they were smaller, with stubby fingers and bitten nails that weren't her own. While trying to make sense of staring down at her past self, a puff of black smoke flowed by her cheek, burning her nostrils—noxious and choking—carrying the unmistakable scent of burning wood and synthetics drifted out through the opening in the wall. The classroom walls shimmered with heat. Desks that hadn't existed moments before now appeared, arranged in neat rows, some already catching fire at their edges. A chalkboard materialized behind her, covered with cursive letters that melted and ran down the surface like wax.

"I'm coming!" her other self-called.

Meanwhile, Betsy and Tammy had just finished placing Mrs. Carmichael in the walk-in freezer and were heading back to the nurse's station when Betsy noticed the makeshift danger sign lying on the floor in front of room 115. Tammy followed her to the door, and Betsy glanced down at the fallen banner.

A lot of good that did, Betsy thought.

"This is the room Kate's car is stuck in the wall," Betsy said.

"So, who's inside?" Tammy said.

Betsy knocked on the door.

Behind the door, Betsy heard a little girl call for help and assumed it was Cloreese.

From inside the room, Beth heard Betsy calling for her from outside the door. The lights went out for a second then came back on. When Beth turned to look, she noticed a gap in the floor with flames leaping up from the opening that hadn't been there before; the exact spot where Jack's dead body had lain. The room was wrong: linoleum tiles to vinyl composition tile that became warped planking. Her classroom had transformed into the deck of a ship. Night had returned. A life ring buoy hung on the wall, resembling a large donut with the word Titanic arching along the top and London curving along the bottom. Right away she linked the famous last words a White Star Line employee made at the ship's launch in 1911 to the sinking ship.

The stupid man said that not God himself could sink this ship, she thought. What a foolish thing to say.

What stood between her and the door was an opening in the floor with protruding flames. The smoke stung her eyes, forcing her to close them for a moment, sending tears streaming down her cheeks. The temporary relief from the sting was immeasurable in such a short time. The floor shifted, throwing off her balance. She fell to her hands and knees, still a few feet from the flaming mouth. Her body leaned toward the hole, and the heat brushed against her forehead like the scorching sun on a beach, cooking her skin. She screamed. Kate's car teetered just inches closer to her. She screamed again. Then the room tilted in the opposite direction, sending Kate's vehicle over the edge of the ship into the dark sea. Beth's body slid, like a wet fish, toward the mangled railing where Kate's car had gone over. She grabbed hold of a piece of cold iron, preventing herself from plunging into the ocean.

Which ocean it was or where she was located was anyone's guess, but she could only assume that if she were on the Titanic, the water would be icy cold. Clinging to the railing, she hung there over the steep drop, her legs dangling in the open air. She gazed across the full length of the nursing home. The west wing now became the bow of the ship, still intact, with the brick walls moving with the motion of the ship beneath. She dared a look down, expecting to see Moby Dick. She blinked a couple of times with uncertainty, questioning her own senses. Waves crashed just below her against the side of the ship, sending salty water in her face. She could taste the salt on her lips.

"Help me," she screamed.

Through the opening in the rails, she spotted Betsy rushing through the door, halting just inches from the fiery hole in the floor. Tammy still had the stretcher they used for Mrs. Carmichael. Betsy kneeled and helped Tammy balance the stretcher across the burning chasm, bridging it by faith.

Beth looked forward toward the bow again and caught sight of a massive iceberg drifting toward the nursing home ship.

"Hurry," Beth said.

Betsy stepped with caution, crossing over the burning pit, using the stretcher as a shield. Although the stretcher was stiff and sturdy, it was wood, and once it caught fire, they would only have a few minutes before it completely burned through, sending the flaming board into the pit along with their chances of survival. Betsy reached Beth first, grabbing her right arm. Just as she secured her grip, a giant octopus's arm, covered in slimy suckers, emerged from the water and coiled around Beth's left ankle. Beth's face contorted in agony as she screamed. Tammy paused in disbelief, watching as the iceberg drifted closer. The nursing-home ship creaked beneath them.

"Help me!" Betsy shouted to Tammy.

Beth's arms and legs screamed with fatigue.

Tammy snapped back into focus. She reached into her scrub coat pocket and pulled out a surgical knife. With a swift motion, she cut the octopus's arm, blood spraying onto the three of them and the ship's deck. The octopus released its grip. Tammy grasped Beth's left arm, and together with Betsy, they heaved Beth over the railing to safety. The severed octopus tentacle still twitched beside her. Betsy and Tammy helped Beth to her feet. It was a harrowing battle against the elements, an epic struggle between human and sea creature, and in the midst of it all, the three women clung to each other in a fierce and unbreakable bond of friendship and survival. But the momentary victory was short-lived. The iceberg loomed larger now, its jagged peak glistening like a massive tooth in the moonlight. Beth's ankle throbbed where the octopus had gripped her, the suction marks already red welts against her pale skin. Tammy wiped the creature's blood from her hands onto her scrubs, leaving dark smears across the once-pristine fabric.

"I thought octopuses lived in warm waters," Betsy said.

"It varies by species," Beth said. "Some, like the Antarctic octopus, thrive in cold waters."

"Does any of this make sense to you?" Tammy said. "For crying out loud, the nursing home is a ship in the middle of the ocean.

"Look," Beth said.

The stretcher was burning faster than expected. The belts were the first to go.

"We need to hurry," Betsy said, doubting whether it would support their weight.

"Yeah, need I remind you that an iceberg is on a collision course with the nursing home?" Tammy said.

Beth went first, followed by Betsy. But after Betsy's step onto the wooden spine board that was meant to carry the deceased to the walk-in freezer, it snapped in two. Beth grabbed Betsy's sleeve and yanked her hard towards the door. Tammy stayed behind, on the side where the octopus's blood mingled with the salty waves reaching for the edge of the deck.

"What do you want?" Tammy yelled at no one in particular. The ship shifted again, trying to throw Tammy into the flames. But she anticipated it and jumped. Beth and Betsy caught her, pulling her to safety.

"I guess all those days at the gym paid off," Tammy said with a grin.

"This must mean you're not next to die," Beth said to Tammy.

Betsy opened the door, and the three of them collapsed in the hallway, exhausted.

"I'm never going back in there," Beth said. "Ever." She emphasized.

Betsy was trying to catch her breath.

"Why did you go in there in the first place?" Betsy said. "Especially alone."

"I had reason to suspect that Kate's car broke the fire hydrant, leading us to think it was raining outside," Beth said.

"After what I just witnessed," Tammy said, "ignoring any impossibility could land you in the freezer."

"If I could prove there's no storm, then it would mean your son is still alive," Beth said to Betsy.

"Whatever this thing is, it is playing tricks on us to make us all go off the deep end. We have to keep our sanity," Tammy said.

Betsy took hold of the makeshift danger sign and reattached it across the threshold.

"My intuition tells me that my son is still alive," Betsy said. "I can't explain it; I just know."

CHAPTER 42

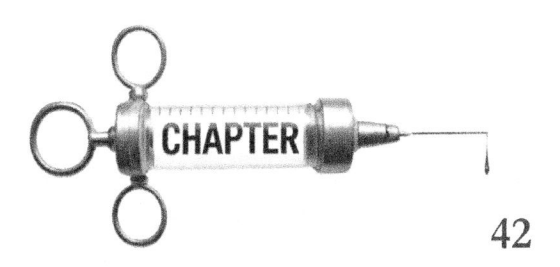

The television flickered to life at the nurse's station, the picture crystal clear and the volume cranked to its highest setting. Betsy, Beth, and Tammy rushed over to lower the volume, hoping not to disturb any residents who might be sleeping.

"Where's Missy?" Betsy said.

"We'd better keep what happened in room 115 to ourselves," Tammy said. "She wouldn't believe it."

Betsy found the remote and turned the volume down to a more moderate level.

"Hi, I'm Michelle Piper. On tonight's local news, eight people have died at the Weather the Storm Nursing Home. Rose Windslow died during transport to Lakeside Memorial Hospital. Sources said that a nurse administered the wrong medication, leading to her untimely death."

"That's not what happened," Betsy said.

"Although this investigation has led authorities to the suspicion of foul play; the nurse in question committed suicide by hanging herself with her own panties. Jack Clementine, the maintenance man, was in the parking lot to go home when struck by a car and died as a result of a jealous confrontation between two nurses he was allegedly involved with."

"The nerve of that news station," Tammy said.

"This is fake news," Betsy said.

"It's him," Beth said.

"Who?" Tammy said, glancing between the two women, confusion etched on her face.

"John Doe," Beth said, her eyes narrowing. "He's causing all this."

"Sources have reported that Betsy, who has been struggling with depression after her son Blake Monaghan's recent death, went on a killing spree, locking one nurse in the freezer to die and setting a resident named Baxter Evans on fire without mercy. Another resident, whom we have not identified, was wearing a DNR bracelet, which stands for Do Not Resuscitate. She received multiple shocks to her healthy heart with a defibrillator until she died a cruel death. The prosecutor handling the case is confident that Betsy will face the death penalty once the jury delivers a guilty verdict."

"He's the storm," Beth said.

"A man controlling the weather. I've read about cloud seeding, where someone can fly a plane into a cloud and release silver iodide and solid carbon dioxide like dry ice; it's a technique used for weather modification to induce rain."

"He isn't a man," Beth said. "He's the one who set the school building on fire back in 1966."

"I'm not even going to ask you how you know that," Tammy said.

Betsy looked confused.

"You're not letting this get to you, are you?" Tammy said to Betsy.

"Michelle Piper said she," Betsy said.

"Who?" Beth said.

"The anchorwoman, she said 'she' when talking about the resident who died from a heart attack," Betsy said.

"What are you getting at?" Tammy said.

"When I heard her mention the misuse of a defibrillator, I first thought she was referring to Rosslyn Winters, who died of a heart attack. He was screaming that his legs were on fire until his heart failed and he gave up the ghost. But the anchorwoman said she died of shocking the heart. Who is she?" Betsy said.

"I'm telling you, John Doe is a liar," Beth said. "He isn't human."

"I'm going to find out," Betsy said.

"How are you going to do that?" Tammy said.

"Follow me," Betsy said.

She stood up and walked down the hall, with Beth and Tammy following.

CHAPTER 43

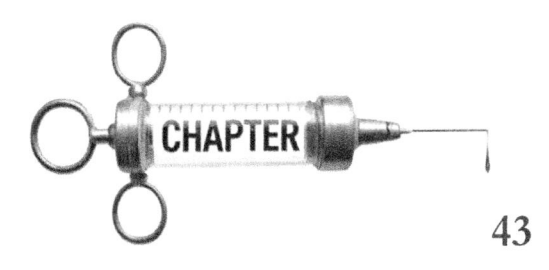

Missy regained consciousness on the cold linoleum after being knocked out, lying on the floor in a daze. She blinked a few times and turned her head to the right, glancing under Mrs. Julia Shadwack's bed. To her left were the swivel casters of an adjustable over-bed table that Mrs. Shadwack had once used for her meals. Now, however, she was dead. The memory of why she was on the floor flooded back to Missy. Out of anger, she pressed the paddles to her temples with no intention of triggering an electric shock wave into her brain, but when she yelled out in fury, the last thing she remembered was her vision went black. She recalled losing herself in a fit of rage. She had attempted to resuscitate Julia using the paddles. Somehow, the mechanism took over recharging and firing without stopping on its own, either by a malfunction like a short circuit or some unexplainable phenomenon she couldn't include in the incident report without sounding crazy. The repeated discharges caused Mrs. Shadwack's heart to stop.

Missy's temples throbbed, with minor burns evident on her skin, and the reek of stale urine hit her nostrils like a soiled diaper.

When she lifted her head to look at her feet, she noticed a little girl standing by the door.

"Are you Cloreese?" Missy said.

The little girl nodded. She wore a white dress, simple and old-fashioned, with a hem that hovered just beneath her knees. Her arms hung at her sides, hands loose, fingers slightly curled.

"I think we're all going to die," Missy said in a whisper, dry mouth, and her jaw quivering.

"Not everyone," Cloreese said.

"What about me?" Missy said. "Am I going to die?"

Cloreese nodded.

"Most definitely," Cloreese said.

"Well, you don't have to be so cheery about it," Missy said.

Cloreese remained silent.

"I don't want to die," Missy said. "What can I do?"

"Pray," Cloreese said.

"But I'm not religious," Missy said.

"Too bad, so sad," Cloreese said as she turned and skipped off out of the room.

"I believe that God exists, though," Missy said, raising her voice to catch up with the little girl. "Does that count?"

"Even the devil believes God exists, but he, like you, chooses not to follow," Cloreese said, her voice echoing as she moved further down the hallway.

Missy glanced once more between her legs and spotted the defibrillator paddles resting in her pool of urine. The machine whined like before, then lit up with a green glow, indicating it was ready and willing to fire. She put her heels to work, scooting her butt away from the urine. She waited for the shock, but it never came. The green light died out.

CHAPTER 44

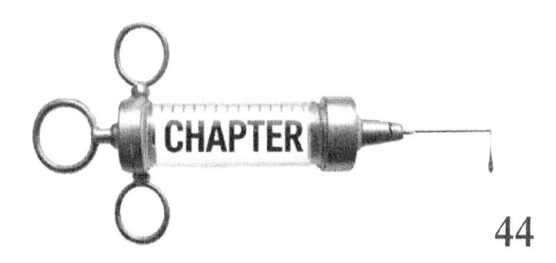

Betsy, Beth, and Tammy wheeled John Doe's bed toward the x-ray room. As they approached the chapel doorway, the bed moved away from the opening, much like two magnets with the same pole repelling each other when brought close. The bed shoved Beth against the wall, pressing firm against her hip. She screamed in pain. Once the bed passed the chapel entrance, the wheels resumed their normal forward motion as the external force disappeared.

"What just happened?" Beth said to Betsy and Tammy.

"I felt it too," Betsy said.

"It wasn't me," Tammy said.

Beth lifted her shirt to reveal a red mark on her hip.

"That's going to bruise," Tammy said.

Beth thought about the incident for a moment as they continued wheeling John Doe down the hallway toward the x-ray room.

Once inside the room, Betsy placed her lead initials on the x-ray film cassette, right beneath John Doe for an abdominal x-ray, while Beth and Tammy waited for her in the control room. Betsy retreated to the control room and set the exposure. The breathing mechanism attached to the ventilator pump maintained a rhythm, forcing John Doe's chest to inflate and collapse. Betsy watched and listened, then pressed the start button as the bellows fully expanded. The machine whined. A beam of invisible radiation passed through John Doe's body, and through the film, capturing an image of any dense internal structures.

"X-rays don't lie," Tammy said. "It'll show whether he's male or female, regardless of how he looks on the outside."

"Really?" Beth said, still cradling her hip. She wanted to focus on anything but the pain in her side.

"You didn't know that?" Betsy said to Beth. "It's basic anatomy. The pelvis gives it away."

Betsy and Tammy exchanged glances with Beth.

"You care to refresh my memory," Beth said.

"A male pelvis is thick and heavy, with a smaller inlet than a female's, which has a heart shape. A good way to remember that is: the way to a man's heart is through his pelvis," Betsy said.

"The female pelvis is thin, with a wide, oval, and round superior pelvic aperture, which is ideal for childbirth. The male coccyx is rigid and has little curvature, while the female's is flexible, movable, and has a curve. So, keep in mind that females have more curves," Tammy said.

"Now that you mention it, I do recall the part about the heart," Beth said.

Betsy and Tammy exchanged glances, eyebrows raised.

They all watched as the film emerged from the developing machine.

Betsy held it up to the X-ray film light, squinting. Something was wrong.

"Well, there's no bones about it," she said.

Tammy stepped closer, expecting to see the familiar gray-scale fog of a human skeleton and viscera, the ghostly signature of a living body.

Instead, the film showed thousands of white maggots, as if the body on the table contained nothing more than little legless worm-like larvae. But there was something else: three words, formed in bone-looking font, perfectly arranged in the space where the ribcage should have been.

Trick or Treat

Tammy snatched the film. "Is this a prank? Is this some kind of joke?" she said. "This can't be right, can it?"

"Do I look like I'm laughing?" Betsy said, her expression serious. "You can see my marker."

"Could the film have been tampered with or altered?" Beth said.

"Who would risk their job to do such a thing and for what reason?" Betsy said. "The prankster would have to witness the hoax to benefit from it, wouldn't they?"

"I don't believe any of us would do such a thing," Beth said.

"Is the film old or expired?" Tammy said.

"With the number of x-rays we do here, there's no way the film could sit around long enough to expire," Betsy said. "You know just as well as I do that the inventory is always recorded and checked with strict scrutiny. But for the sake of authenticity and to rule out any errors, let's retake the X-ray."

Betsy took a second X-ray having the same results. The three of them stared at the X-ray for a minute, unwilling to be the first to look away. They each searched for an explanation, cycling through the possibilities—old and outdated, defective film, a hoax—but none stood up to scrutiny. John Doe's body beneath the sheet was as motionless as before.

"See my initials in white?" Betsy said. "The film and the developing process are working properly."

"He's not human," Beth said, and the words hung in the air like radio static.

For a moment, none of them moved.

Tammy's face hardened.

"We'll just see about that," she said.

"What are you planning to do?" Beth said.

"Watch and learn, sweethearts," Tammy said.

She raised the sheet off John Doe's left foot and with the same scalpel she had used to cut the octopus's arm off; she made a deep vertical incision down the center of John Doe's foot, slicing the flesh just below his toes all the way to his heel, but there was no blood. No resistance either; the tissue parted like warm wax.

"Oh my gosh," Beth said. She felt suddenly cold, as though the room had been drained of air.

"Look," Betsy said.

As they gazed at the injury, the wound, already closing, had healed within seconds. Flesh reformed, leaving no scar, no mark—nothing at all. John Doe's foot was just as it had been before the incision.

The overhead lights flickered.

"What do you think he is?" Betsy said. Her mouth moved as she turned to speak. Tammy and Beth saw her lips shape the words, but heard nothing.

"What are you saying?" Tammy said, but her voice was also silent.

"I'm confused," Beth mouthed, with only silence filling the air around them. She looked to Betsy, who was gesturing in a fit of desperation at the door, pointing, mouthing something urgent.

None of them could hear each other's voices. Strangely, they all picked up on the sound of a fax machine printing an incoming message, even though it was located down the hall, far beyond their hearing range.

The lights went out.

Each person searched for something familiar, but it felt like several minutes passed before anyone could find anything. It wasn't for lack of effort; it was as if the room had expanded so much that what should have been a straightforward walk to the door, now became a challenge to navigate because the door was no longer where it was supposed to be.

Beth felt a small hand slip into hers.

It's Cloreese, the little girl, she thought.

Cloreese guided Beth with her left hand. She allowed Cloreese to pull her forward, leading them to Betsy, who took hold of Beth's right hand. Beth recognized it was Betsy because of her habit of biting her nails.

Betsy felt a grip on her right hand that she thought belonged to Tammy. The nails were long like Tammy's, but they felt a little rough.

Whose hand could it be if it wasn't Tammy's? She thought.

They all hoped one of them would find the door, so they could all escape into the light together.

Follow the light to be saved, Beth thought.

Cloreese directed Beth's hand to the doorhandle—a familiar shape, cold metal. Beth opened the door, and she and Betsy stepped out into the hallway. Beth looked back and saw the darkness behind her, dense and silent, swallowing up the room and the furniture and everything that should have been there. The light in the hallway didn't penetrate the X-ray room. It was as if the void hovered at the threshold.

"How did you manage to find the door?" Betsy said.

"Cloreese guided me," Beth said, scanning the hallway. It was empty except for the two of them and the long, echoing stretch to the exit. "Where's Tammy?"

"She was just behind me, holding onto my right hand," Betsy said.

"Are you sure?" Beth said, her voice growing in urgency.

Betsy looked at her right hand—the same hand she believed Tammy had been holding. "I don't know what happened," she said. "The lights went out; I felt Tammy's long fingernails in my hand, and then…" She opened her palm and found a piece of hard candy resting there. She let it drop to the floor. It made a loud clink when it hit the linoleum.

"After everything we've experienced, how can we be sure of anything?" she said. "At least we have our voices back."

"We need to go back in and help her," Beth said. She stepped toward the door, but it had already swung shut behind them in a rather unfriendly manner. John Doe wanted them out to have Tammy alone with him. The door handle refused to budge regardless of how hard she pulled.

They tried to open the door again, but it wouldn't budge.

"You stay here in case Tammy gets out with the help of Cloreese or on her own," Betsy said.

"Where are you going?" Beth said.

"I'm going to get an axe," Betsy said. "One way or another, I'm getting into that room."

Beth watched as Betsy walked to the end of the hallway and turned right. She was alone. She hugged herself, feeling the ache in her hip from earlier, the spot where the bed had shoved her into the wall. It was already throbbing, swelling against the waistband of her scrub pants. After a moment, Beth pivoted, looking the other way down the long stretch of hallway when Betsy came around the corner from the left, approaching her from behind. Had Beth been looking, she'd have seen one Betsy turn to the right and another Betsy return from the left. The person resembling Betsy seemed unlike herself. It was the footsteps she heard that were different. She craned her neck and saw Betsy—or someone who looked like her—approaching with even steady steps and a blank expression, not the quick determined, angry strides of Betsy that had left her standing here alone just moments before.

"Beth," Betsy's double said.

Beth jumped, not expecting her back so soon.

"Where's the axe?" Beth said.

"Never mind that right now," Betsy's double said. "I found Missy, and she's going to help me."

"Oh, okay," Beth said. "Where is she?"

"She went to get the axe," Betsy's double said. "Here, take these." She pressed two small tablets into Beth's hand.

"What are they?" Beth said, puzzled by why Betsy had shifted her focus from getting an axe to handing her pills with no apparent reason. She studied the pills, both identical: round, white. She wondered if they were even legal.

"They'll help with your menstrual pain and bloating," Betsy's double said. "You should take them right away."

Beth stiffened, the chill of dread skating along her spine.

"How did you know I'm on my period?" she said. She tried to keep her voice casual, but the question sounded accusatory even to her own ears.

"It's not a big secret, Beth; grow up," Betsy's double said. "You can smell it in the restroom. Like something died."

"Maybe I'll take them later if I feel any pain," Beth said, tucking the tablets into her front pocket. She noticed Betsy's double watching her closely with a predator's patience.

"Suit yourself; I'm just trying to help," Betsy's double said. "I suspect no one told you, but you're showing on your backside. Go to the restroom and take care of yourself, clean yourself up."

She observed that Betsy's demeanor had shifted from being stressed and focused on helping Tammy to calm and attentive towards her instead. It made little sense. Beth frowned, reaching around to check, feeling the sticky warmth of the accident forming a stain on her scrubs. Her face contorted in disgust. She couldn't help but feel self-conscious, aware of the subtle but distinct odor emanating from her. The shame was disproportionate to the situation, but she nodded; unwilling to argue. Trusting her instincts, Beth decided it was best to play along—for now. She would go to the restroom, she decided, where she could at least lock the door and gather her thoughts. The walk down the hallway felt longer than it should have. Every few paces, Beth glanced back, half expecting Betsy's double to follow her or for some new threat to emerge from the wall. She wasn't certain that the weird-acting Betsy, or John Doe, didn't have something to do with her little accident. Once in the restroom, she checked her reflection in the mirror, turned around, and examined her backside: a crescent of blood had seeped through the fabric. By the time she finished cleaning herself up, she was determined to have figured out her next move.

CHAPTER 45

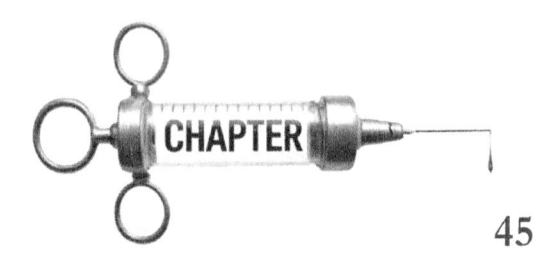

Tammy's eyes adjusted to the darkness when slivers of light began filtering into the room through small gaps in the windows near the ceiling. The beams had sneaked in through a few broken chunks of glass, damage she attributed to vandals who had nothing better to do than hurl rocks at an abandoned building.

Was it abandoned? She thought.

Dust particles danced in the rays of sunlight streaming down. A film resembling cigarette tar obscured the visibility through the other windows, casting a dull tint over the sunlight outside.

It was a sign that morning had arrived. Just moments earlier, she couldn't see her hand in front of her face, but now the sunlight had restored her vision.

Am I still at the nursing home, or somewhere else? She thought. *Is the morning staff here to take over?*

She scanned the room for Beth and Betsy, but they were gone. She didn't hold it against them; for all she knew, they might still be in the X-ray room in another dimension. Tammy was alone with John Doe. He still appeared to be in a coma, harmless; but she knew better. She has had her share of violent men, but this man topped them all. She never could have imagined a man who had never slapped her, never raped her, never beat her, never belittled her, never argued and used inappropriate language like that of the ignorant, yet to be the most dangerous man she's ever encountered.

The room wasn't as it was when she came in with Beth and Betsy. What had once been an x-ray room had transformed into an abandoned space of a rundown psychiatric ward, like the one Beth had threatened to send Stella to. The walls had padding up to eight feet, with sections of pillows about two feet wide. Under the windows, the padding had stained with mold in various areas. Other parts showed signs of mice gnawing through the fabric, leaving lumps of stuffing protruding like a wounded teddy bear. The paint on the walls, two feet above the padding, was an aged light green, flaking off in places. Some of the peeling was severe, curling up like Velcro rollers used for styling bouffant hairdos. An old Cape Bristol ventilator was providing air for John Doe, the bellows collapsed and expanded with the rise and fall of his chest. The room was hot; Tammy felt sticky. She couldn't shake the feeling of filth with all the tacky dust particles floating in the air, adhering to her clammy skin as if her body was a magnet for mosquitoes. She unbuttoned her blouse, revealing beads of sweat trailing down between her breasts. She felt the perspiration pooling in the small of her back, forming droplets that ran down the crack of her butt in rivulets. The damp, musty air was stale, permeated with a foul smell of old urine. Debris littered the floor.

There was no sound of a storm, she thought.

The linoleum tiles were different—these were the nine-inch by nine-inch tiles used years ago, notorious for containing asbestos. Some tiles had cracks, and others had broken corners with detached pieces scattered about. The floor's debris resembled accumulated sawdust from a wood shop, as though no one had swept the area in years. The floor also seemed to have had padding, that someone must've ripped it away, leaving crusted remains of glue. She noticed that John Doe's respirator was functioning, even with the electric cord's male plug lying on the floor disconnected from any power source.

Curiosity overwhelmed Tammy about why the room was empty except for old newspapers strewn about. She stooped and claimed the nearest one to satisfy her need-to-know appetite.

Harper Gazette

NURSING HOME RESIDENTS BECOME VICTIMS OF INCOMPETENT ORDERLIES AFTER MANDATORY EVACUATION ORDER WAS DISREGARDED DESPITE FEDERAL STATE OF EMERGENCY WARNINGS.

Another headline stated:

CATEGORY FOUR STORM WITH WINDS EXCEEDING 130 MPH LEAVES A TRAIL OF DESTRUCTION ACROSS THE STATE, CLAIMING HUNDREDS OF LIVES IN NURSING HOMES.

She continued reading, feeling disgusted by her discoveries:

NURSING HOME REACHED TEMPERATURES ABOVE 108 DEGREES. HEALTHCARE WORKERS CHARGED WITH MANSLAUGHTER.

THE INDEPENDENCE SENTINEL reported:

NURSING HOME OWNER FACES 35 COUNTS OF NEGLIGENT HOMICIDE. SOME VICTIMS' BODY TEMPERATURES REACHED 108 DEGREES, ACCORDING TO RESPONDING PARAMEDICS.

She picked up another article crumpled into a ball. Carefully, she unfolded it to avoid tearing the fragile paper.

OIL COMPANIES EVACUATED SEVERAL PLATFORMS, A PRIORITY CONSIDERED WORTH SAVING, UNLIKE THE RESIDENTS IN NURSING HOMES, WHO WERE NOT SO FORTUNATE.

Amidst the scattered tumbleweeds of neglected newspapers, Tammy managed to piece together a sad picture of humanity's psyche, marked by a lack of compassion with the increase of greed. She wondered how many individuals had bought copies of these papers only to skip over the stories exposing greed and corruption, flipping to the sports section instead. Someone might have given a fresh coat of paint to aging cars with some of these papers taped to the windows. Who could say for certain? As far as she was concerned, the stories could be fabricated, yet deep down, she doubted that was the case. As her gaze drifted over the obituaries, her skepticism passed away.

Tammy L. Bisset, aged 27, from Bohemian Grove, passed away on October 31st, 2025, at the Weather the Storm Nursing Home, where she worked as a nurse. However, after she harmed a resident just to observe him bleed, her coworkers restrained her and subjected her to electric shock therapy, resulting in her death from an overload to the brain. She divorced and died alone, without children. No services will take place because no one cared for her except her Labrador Retriever, and funeral homes do not allow dogs. She resembled the elderly woman in the supermarket with a leaky bladder, leaving behind a trail of stale urine, and you hoped to avoid eye contact because you didn't want to engage in a conversation.

That's so mean, she thought.

The moment she moved for the door, an electric cord that had come alive, looped itself with serpentine precision around her ankle. She hadn't even registered the contact before it yanked her off balance, pitching her forward with such force that her knees met the filthy linoleum hard enough to send shock waves of pain up her thighs. She clawed at the floor for purchase, using her shoes as brakes. She was being dragged towards the bed. The cord tightened, constricting; its cold plastic pressed deeper into her flesh with every inch she tried to crawl away. She struggled to lever herself up, but the cord only wound tighter, pulsing, as if alive, as if it could sense her resistance and drew strength from her pain. She planted her shoes against the floor and tried to kick backwards, but the motion only succeeded in flipping her nurse's skirt up over her hips, exposing her white bikini panties, streaked now with grime and a film resembling aged brown soap scum that stained the tiles. The tarnish-like stains on her sweaty palms and the abrasions on her knees from the broken linoleum tiles only intensified her struggle. The more she fought, the more injuries she sustained, leaving a trail of blood on the floor where her knees scraped against the uneven surface, making it slippery. Humiliation stung her, as if even now she could not bear to be seen like this, reduced to an animal scrambling for survival. Desperately, she fought to escape, like a baby trying to swim away from the cannula suction tube in its mother's uterus that threatened to tear it apart.

She could feel the cord's progress as it snaked up her leg, twisting with monstrous intent. It pushed beneath the waistband of her panties and wriggled upward over her bellybutton, slick with sweat and dust, moving as if guided by a mind of its own. She didn't need intuition to tell her the cord was heading toward her throat. In a frantic, senseless motion, she rolled to her side and pressed her weight against the cord, trying to pin it down in an attempt to halt its movement. She used her heels to gain traction while she felt for her scalpel in her jacket pocket. She snatched it with a trembling hand, coming close to dropping it once as her slick palms failed to get a purchase on the tiny steel handle. At that instant, the cord constricted again, this time around her waist. She was fighting to get away the only means she knew how. Her knees stung as sweat seeped into her wounds. Beneath her skirt, the electric cord moved with the force of octopus tentacles, like the one that grabbed ahold of Beth's ankle. It was as powerful as a creature fighting for survival. With the scalpel gripped tight in her right hand, she glanced down at her bra, noticing movement between her breasts. But to her shock, it wasn't the electric cord; it was an umbilical cord. Looking further down her body, she saw that the electric cord still held her ankle. That explained why she hadn't felt the cord slip beneath the hem that clung to her right thigh—as a man's hand would do. She was ticklish in that spot, and even though this was no laughing matter she would've noticed. She recalled confiding in Missy a couple of years prior about her leave of absence because of a pregnancy loss caused by the umbilical cord wrapping around her baby's neck. Now, she was experiencing the same struggle her baby had once faced. She was the fetus, a helpless thing, and the cord was suffocating her just as it had suffocated her child. She attempted to pull it away from her neck just enough to insert her scalpel into the gap, but it constricted tighter and tighter, like a boa constrictor. She worried that if she cut toward her neck and the blade went too far, she could sever her carotid artery. If that happened it would be lights out for sure. The umbilical cord was too slippery for her to get a grip. Her hands were sweaty. She tried with all her power to hold on to the scalpel. Her face turned blue, and her legs weakened. She wondered if this was how her baby had felt—panicked, choking, alone—when it strangled inside her. It was a stupid, sentimental thought, but it overwhelmed her as the world narrowed to a bright white tunnel.

If I'm going to die regardless, I might as well go out fighting, she thought as she angled the scalpel blade against the umbilical cord constricting her throat. But before she could make her cut against this monster, her arms collapsed with lifelessness. The scalpel slipped from her sweaty grasp, clinking on the floor. Her thigh muscles jerked with spasms at first, then came to a halt. She was close to death's door, but she wasn't dead—not yet.

CHAPTER 46

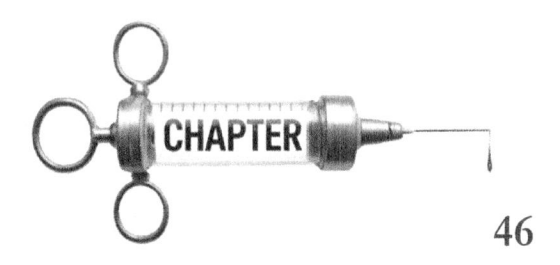

Betsy returned to the x-ray room wielding a red-handled fire axe, but Beth was nowhere to be found. She pondered whether Beth had entered the room, which meant she would have to save two people instead of one. As she prepared to swing the axe with all her strength, the door clicked open. Light spilled out from the other side, and Betsy used the axe handle to push the door wide.

"Beth, Tammy, are you in there?" Betsy said.

The room was as it were when Betsy, Beth, and Tammy brought John Doe there, except for the metal table, which held John Doe for his x-ray, now lay Tammy's body. John Doe sat in a wheelchair, his chin resting on his chest, and the only indication of him being alive was the steady sound of the ventilator assisting his breathing.

He must still be in a coma, Betsy thought.

John Doe remained motionless, the same as before.

Betsy turned her attention to Tammy, who wasn't responding to her being there. Tammy lay restrained, with her ankles pulled apart and secured by straps to the sides of the steel bed. She wore a hospital gown, but it offered little coverage as the room started to rain. It was as though a massive cloud had formed above them. The sight of rain falling from the ceiling, despite the dry ceiling tiles, was a supernatural phenomenon. Betsy's white nurse's uniform quickly soaked through, becoming transparent, revealing her white bra and bikini panties with pink peonies floral pattern. She was oblivious to her appearance; her focus was solely on rescuing her friend.

Standing in the accumulating water, Betsy watched in disbelief as Tammy was prepared for electric shock therapy. Someone placed electrodes on each side of Tammy's head, and as Betsy moved closer, a jolt of electricity surged through Tammy's muscles, forcing her spine to arch in a painful, unnatural position.

"Stop it," Betsy said to John Doe.

He didn't lift his head or show any sign of awareness.

"Is she still alive?" Betsy said aloud as if expecting a response.

Another shock jolted Tammy's body, forcing her spine to arch again. After the convulsion ceased, Tammy lay still on the table, lifeless as before.

The EKG printer began making noises, and two words printed out: NOT NOW.

Betsy buzzed the nurses' station, her face dripping with rain.

"Missy, are you there?" Betsy said. "Can anyone hear me? I need one milligram of epinephrine. Please, I'm in the X-ray room."

As she spoke, water sprayed from her lips, resembling spittle. Her eyelids blinked, reacting to the rain falling on her face.

Meanwhile, Missy was at the nurse's station, applying orange Halloween makeup to her face and chest, complete with black square teeth detailing around her mouth and large triangle eyes painted like a jack-o'-lantern.

"You're awful needy," Missy said to no one. "Where were you when I needed help with Mrs. Shadwack? Because of you, she's dead."

Tammy flatlined.

Fueled by fury, Betsy raised the axe and advanced toward John Doe, preparing to swing it at him.

"You monster," Betsy said.

While staring at John Doe, she heard her son Blake's voice emerge from Tammy's dead lips.

"Mommy, are you going to hurt me?" Blake's voice spoke from Tammy's mouth.

Betsy glanced from Tammy to John Doe and then fled the room.

She carried the axe back to the nursing station, leaning it against the wall.

When she arrived at the nurses' station, she found it deserted. She wondered where Missy had gone.

CHAPTER 47

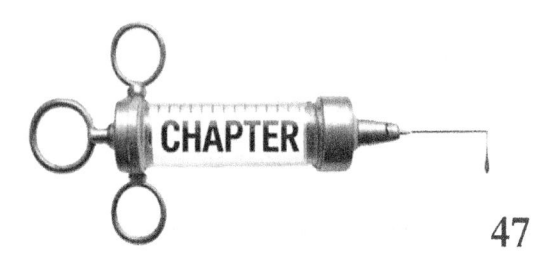

Beth stepped out of the restroom and headed towards the last spot she had seen Betsy when Missy's voice echoed from down the hall. Initially, she walked past the physical fitness room but then paused, retreated a few steps back, and peered inside. There was Missy, bouncing up and down on a stability ball like a child. At first, Beth wondered if this was part of Missy's nightly routine, as she hadn't known her prior to tonight. She wasn't sure if Missy was working on her thighs, preparing for horseback riding, or strengthening her back for better posture. But the sight of Missy's skin, entirely covered in makeup from her hairline down to her collarbone, caused the hairs on her arms to stand up. The layers formed a jack-o'-lantern appearance, while Missy's red hair in pigtails draped over her shoulders. The hallway lights were enough to see Missy's grim expression in the dimly lit room, where her exaggerated black square teeth extended well past the corners of her mouth, reaching up to her cheeks. The base color of her makeup was pumpkin orange, with matching black triangles framing each eye and her nose. Beth felt shocked at Missy's appearance. To heighten the eerie feeling that something was off, Missy fixed her gaze on Beth, yet it seemed as if she stared through her rather than at her. Moreover, Missy kept repeating a phrase over and over, reminiscent of an old scratched vinyl record that keeps looping a few annoying bars of music until someone lifted the needle.

"Trick or treat," Missy said in repetition, her voice monotone.

Then, a bolt of lightning flashed its brilliant light, illuminating the room through the skylights, casting a spotlight on Missy's legs. With the flash, Beth's gaze shifted from Missy's face to her legs.

Beth gasped, frozen in the doorway.

Blood trickled down Missy's shins, appearing as a mutilated pair of fishnet stockings, while her long red-painted fingernails were digging into her skin at the knees. At first, Beth didn't notice Missy's injuries because she stared in disbelief at Missy's makeup, wondering when she had found the time to apply it and for what reason. Surely, she didn't want to alarm the residents, especially those with weak hearts.

"Missy, are you okay?" she said, trying to get through to her as Missy continued her chant, ignoring Beth as if she weren't there.

Betsy's face emerged from the shadows behind Beth's left shoulder, close enough to whisper in her ear.

"No, she's not alright," Betsy said. "She's teetered on the brink of insanity, wouldn't you agree? Like batty, cuckoo."

Beth jumped, almost peeing her panties.

Betsy grabbed Beth by the upper arm and guided her to the side of the doorway right outside the physical fitness room. As they moved, Beth glanced back at Missy just as the lights flickered off and then on again for a brief moment, following a clap of thunder; long enough for Beth to catch a glimpse of Missy's eyes in the darkness.

"Wait," Beth said.

"What?" Betsy said.

"Did you notice her eyes?" Beth said.

"What about them?" Betsy said.

"When the lights went out... her eyes were glowing red," Beth said.

"John Doe has got to her," Betsy said.

"She's changed," Beth said.

"She's unstable and could pose a danger to herself or the others here," Betsy said.

"No, I mean... while I agree, I was referring to how she's changed her clothes," Beth said.

Missy was now wearing the shirt with two cartoon ghosts wielding syringes above the caption: Boo Boo Crew, I Will Stab You.

"Yeah, she's stolen Tammy's outfit," Betsy said.

"Wait, I'm confused," Beth said.

Though Beth and Betsy could no longer see Missy, they could hear her bouncing.

"Why didn't you stay at the X-ray room like I told you to do?"

"You returned without the axe. When I asked about it, you said Missy was getting it," Beth said.

"Wait, you saw someone who looked like me?" Betsy said.

"If you didn't tell me to go to the restroom and clean myself up—that I was showing on my backside—then yes, it was your lookalike," Beth said.

"I never told you to do that?" Betsy said.

"Then you didn't give me these either, right?" Beth said, extending her right hand to reveal two tablets she had retrieved from her front pocket.

Betsy glanced at the tablets lying in Beth's palm and gasped.

"I would've never given you those to take," Betsy said.

"Your imposter insisted I take them, claiming they would alleviate my menstrual pain and bloating," Beth said.

"Oh my gosh, if you had taken those, we wouldn't be having this conversation right now," Betsy said.

"I sensed something was off, like when you get an uneasy feeling about someone or something," Beth said.

"Right," Betsy said.

"To me, it's spiritual," Beth said. "And right now we're experiencing spiritual warfare."

"What do you mean?" Betsy said.

"John Doe is spreading his evil like wildfire," Beth said. "We must be alert and ready for anything."

"We must kill him and make it look like an accident," Betsy said, whispering and glancing around as if worried about being overheard.

"Are you crazy?" Beth said. "I'm not going to jail for attempted murder." Her voice rose a little higher than a whisper.

"Shhhh, keep your voice down," Betsy said. "You're worried about jail when you should focus on staying alive until the morning light."

"He's our only proof of all this madness. Besides, how do you know the nightmare will end with the dawn?" Beth said.

"A new crew will arrive, and we'll be relieved of our duties and of him," Betsy said, looking in the direction of John Doe.

"After everything that's happened tonight, how can you be sure a pack of hungry apes won't come in the morning, or that we're even in the same dimension we started in? We might end up lost like those who vanished in the Bermuda Triangle. Like…"

"Like what?" Betsy said.

"Not what, but who," Beth said, trying to cover up her slip where she almost revealed being a time-traveling. "Like us. The first-shift nurses could come in and find everyone gone, including the residents. Plus, I'm not comfortable sending the first shift to deal with John Doe—it's like sending lambs to the slaughter. I'm not a coward. We need to take care of him ourselves. This is our watch."

"And how do you propose we don't kill him, keep him from killing us, and still present him to the police in a coma as the one responsible for all those dead bodies piled up in the freezer?"

"I don't know yet," Beth said.

"You said it yourself, Beth, he's not human," Betsy said. "It's like killing an animal except I'd have more sympathy for an animal."

"You can't kill evil," Beth said. "It's like matter; you cannot create it or destroy it—it simply exists as bad energy."

"In order to overcome this problem, we need protection," Betsy said. "As a Boy Scout mom, I'm well-trained in preparedness."

"Why are you soaking wet?" Beth said. "You're getting water on the floor."

"It was raining in the X-ray room," Betsy said.

"The roof is leaking?" Beth said.

"No, the roof is fine," Betsy said, "Never mind. You had to be there."

"Okay. Speaking of water, what we need is some holy water," Beth said.

"What?" Betsy said.

"How do you fight fire?" Beth said.

"Uh, with fire?" Betsy said.

"Normally yes, but in this situation, we're dealing with hellfire from a demon. So, in order to fight this kind of fire, we need holy water," Beth said.

"Then you should go to the chapel and see if you can find some," Betsy said.

"Okay," Beth said.

"You should apply some to your sore side to speed up the healing," Betsy said.

"You don't believe, do you?" Beth said. "Why is it so easy for you not to have faith in good over evil?"

"I just don't know how we're going to pull this off," Betsy said.

"The Doubting Thomas," Beth said.

"Okay, you made your point," Betsy said.

"I'm going to the chapel," Beth said. "If I have to do this myself, I will."

Beth started to walk away.

"Hey, hold on a second. It's like you said, Betsy said. "We're in this together."

She gave Beth a hug.

"We can do this," Beth said.

"I hope you're right," Betsy said.

"What are we going to do about Missy?" Beth said.

"I'm going to give her some haloperidol, a sedative, to calm her down," Betsy said.

"Doesn't a doctor have to approve that?" Beth said.

"Do you see one around?" Betsy said.

"Good point," Beth said.

"Before you go to the chapel, I need your help to move Tammy to the kitchen," Betsy said.

"Oh, no," Beth said. "You found her?"

"Yes," Betsy said, shaking her head to indicate Tammy had died.

"So, she was next," Beth said.

Betsy nodded.

"Let's go," she said, leading the way with Beth following.

Around the corner, Missy stood by the doorway, listening to their conversation. Behind her, the exercise ball continued to bounce as it had when Missy was on it, even though she now stood twenty-three feet away. The top of the ball sank when it hit the ground, as if it still held Missy's weight.

As Betsy and Beth walked down the hall from doorway to doorway, they noticed that all the televisions in the rooms displayed the words "trick or treat" in orange text, moving around on a blank black background. The words would enlarge and then dissipate, while smaller ones would emerge and follow the same repetitive cycle like a screensaver. They passed a retro display case housing an Air-Shield Respirator machine. Despite not being plugged in, the accordion plunger moved up and down as if in use.

Beyond the miniature museum of medical equipment, they came under attack from a medication cart. Drawers opened without human help, and pills flew out like bullets from a machine gun, peppering the walls and floor. Betsy grabbed a discarded dinner tray and held it up like a Roman shield, while Beth stayed close behind. Pills struck it with such force that the tray vibrated in her hands, the clatter echoing down the hallway. Tablets and capsules burst on contact, blooming into chalky white and pastel dust clouds. Some ricocheted over the rim and peppered her forehead, her cheeks, a few even lodging in the outer fold of her ear. They advanced by inches, battered but not beaten. They ducked against the rain of projectiles. Beth, huddled just behind, felt a sharp sting at her thigh, as if a hornet had burrowed beneath her skin. She gasped and pressed her hand against the injury. Betsy was concerned about bruises developing where her clothes offered some protection. Her greater fear was a hit to her eye or neck, which could lead to severe injury or even death if the medication entered their bloodstream. Betsy staggered, losing her balance for a second, but Beth caught her under the arm and helped stabilize her. The pills had left raised welts on Betsy's legs.

In the physical fitness room, Missy roared with laughter. She didn't need to witness the chaos; she somehow just knew what was unfolding. The building was a living, breathing being, with its own network of nerves and bones. Missy tuned into its sensations, feeling the pain and peril as if they were her own. She could taste the airborne chalk of the pills, scattering like ten thousand moth wings.

Simultaneously, Missy could feel Beth's pulse pounding in her temple—the panic, the chilly sweat collecting along the hairline. She perceived Betsy's pain; she could sense the brief spasms of their muscles, the micro-tremors of their fear, the way they braced themselves before lunging from one doorway to the next. She no longer needed to physically watch them to know, for she was in the walls and the lights.

When Beth and Betsy reached the x-ray room, Betsy finally slammed the shield tray against the pill cart, knocking it sideways. The last of the tablets tumbled out with a rattle and a skittering, like a bag of marbles upended onto linoleum. The projectile onslaught had ended. The bombardment from the pill cart ceased. The corridor lay scattered with pastel debris, pill fragments ground into dust beneath their shoes. Judging by the scattered pills in the hallway, the cart must have been empty. Betsy swung open the door, expecting to find John Doe in the wheelchair next to Tammy, but he was gone. The wheelchair was missing as well. John Doe's bed remained in the same spot where they had left it before the lights went out. The rain Betsy mentioned that fell from the ceiling had disappeared, but the room remained damp. Tammy lay sprawled on the metal table; her limbs stretched out in a final display of restraint. Her eyes stared up at the ceiling tiles, wide open; but the light had gone out of them, shocked in a final moment of horror.

Betsy stepped forward, hands trembling, to check on Tammy. She pressed two fingers to the throat, waited, shook her head.

"She's gone," Betsy said.

Beth's eyes filled with tears, and Betsy noticed one trickling down Beth's left cheek.

"Are you okay?" Betsy said.

"I can't—" Beth's voice cracked as she stepped back from the table. Her hands found the wall behind her; fingers splayed against the cool surface as if seeking an anchor in a world that had suddenly become unmoored. "I can't believe she's just gone. And… It's hard for me to imagine Missy stealing her clothes and leaving Tammy like this in a hospital gown. What kind of person does something like this?" she said, not really expecting an answer.

Betsy's rain-soaked uniform clung to her body like a second skin, water still dripping from her hair onto the floor. The weight of Tammy's death pressed against her chest like a heavy stone. Her mind replayed those last moments—Tammy's body arching unnaturally on the table, Blake's voice coming from her dead friend's mouth. A violent shudder ran through her. She moved away from Tammy's body and took hold of Beth's shoulders. "Listen, we need to stay strong. Like you said earlier, this is our watch. We can do this together. Okay?"

Beth nodded. She helped Betsy transfer Tammy's wet body to the bed where John Doe had previously lain. No one could have predicted that they would be pushing the same bed out of the room carrying Tammy's body instead of John Doe's. They intended to use it to transport Tammy's body to the kitchen's walk-in freezer since the wooden stretcher had burned up.

Betsy felt relieved that John Doe wasn't in the room. She didn't know if he was gone from the building, from their lives for good, or if they were being punished with a never-ending nightmare of being stuck with John Doe like a bad tattoo. Just having Beth by her side provided a sense of peace, and that was enough to give her hope.

CHAPTER 48

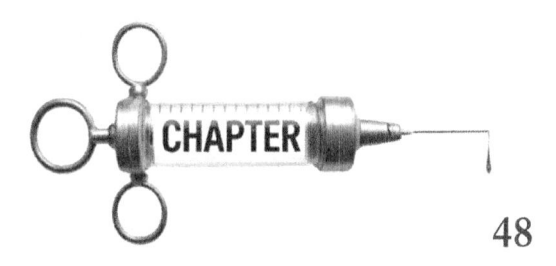

While Betsy occupied herself with preparing a sedative shot for Missy, Beth stepped into the chapel. At the front, a three-foot crucifix hung on the wall. A marble aisle separated six pews, each forty-seven inches wide—three on either side, upholstered in bright red fabric with padded seats and kneelers, as well as bookracks. Beth took in the beauty of the stained-glass windows that illustrated the Stations of the Cross along the sides of the room. She spun around, completing a full circle before gazing back at the entrance she had just come through. Above the door, a sign arched, reading: Greater is he that is in me, than he that is in the world.

Her gaze drifted down to two holy-water fonts, one on each side of the door.

"Looks like you've found what you've been searching for," Cloreese said.

Beth flinched at the sound. She turned and spotted the little girl seated in the front left pew.

"Yes," Beth said. "But how can I use it to rid this evil that has come to this place?"

"Do you remember the story of the Passover?" Cloreese said.

Beth averted her gaze as she tried to recall the details.

"Yes," Beth said. "The Israelites marked their doorposts and lintels with lamb's blood as God instructed, to protect their families from the Angel of Death. When the angel saw the blood, he would pass over the marked houses and continue on, taking the lives of every firstborn son in Egypt."

Beth's eyes landed on a plaque affixed to the end of the pew, with a bible quote from Matthew 18:18 Other pews had similar plaques with quotations from the Holy Bible.

"I suddenly know what I must do," Beth said. "Thank you, Cloreese." She turned back to where she had last seen the little girl, but her excitement dimmed when she realized Cloreese was gone.

Beth approached the font, and using Jennifer's saline solution bottle, which she had taken while passing the nurse's station, filled it with holy water, and began to bless the outside of the doorway with the sign of the cross.

CHAPTER 49

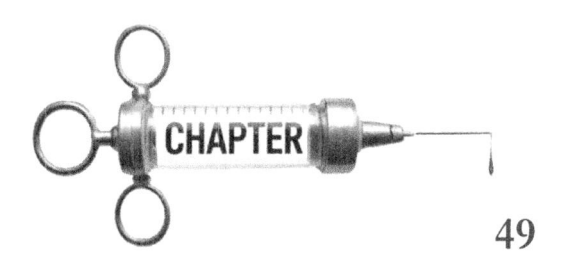

At the nurse's station, Betsy checked the fax machine. The message repeated, "TRICK OR TREAT, NOT COMPLETE, WITHOUT SOME TASTY HUMAN MEAT," printing on the pages.

Missy was squatting under the nursing station's counter as Betsy took a seat in front of her. She placed a syringe containing sedative on the desk. Although she wished to avoid such drastic measures, she felt compelled to act; if she didn't sedate Missy, someone might get hurt—either a resident or Missy herself.

Betsy's wet panties clung to her skin like tight-fitting leggings, and Missy had an unobstructed view of Betsy's wet camel toe through the opening of her skirt. When it comes to being aroused, Missy rejected same-sex interest like magnets repelling each other.

Jack's reflection had told her, "Make her weak and you shall gain strength. Show me you're more loyal to me than she and you will gain my favor."

Jealousy had taken root in her mind, and her intentions were clear: weaken Betsy.

Missy's vantage point, having a full view of Betsy's crotch, meant that Betsy's thighs were too slender to hide her secret area. If Missy were in Betsy's position, wearing the same skirt, her larger thighs would have blocked any view of her hidden parts, which only fueled Missy's resentment.

Little Mrs. Skinny Thighs, she thought. I bet she calls me thunder-thighs behind my back. To her, I'm just a tub of lard.

Jack's voice echoed in her head, urging her to go on and cut Betsy.

Betsy noticed the book Missy had brought in but never read aloud. Out of curiosity, she picked it up and flipped through the first few pages, confusion etched on her face. Realizing the subsequent pages mirrored the first, she thumbed through the rest like a flipbook. A chill ran down her spine, raising the hairs on her arms, similar to the sensation one feels when passing through a cold spot on a calm lake. The words Trick or Treat echoed through the entire book.

Missy reached between Betsy's legs, allowing the scalpel to lead up her short skirt as if the knife had a mind of its own. When her arm was up far enough to appear to an observer in a maternity ward as if Missy was checking Betsy's cervix dilation, she sliced from Betsy's clitoris, slashing through her lace hem hugging her crotch and down her inner thigh. Blood erupted from the fresh wound, a vivid crimson cascade.

Betsy dropped the book, feeling a burning sensation in her right inner thigh. It was worse than the time when she was a kid and sweat entered a cut over her eye. Her brother had passed her a basketball, but her hand reacted slower than the voice inside her head warning that this was going to hurt. She sprang to her feet, her eyes widening as she found Missy crouched beneath the desk, a sinister shadow in the dim light. Lifting the hem of her skirt, Betsy glanced down at her Victoria's Secret laced-waist bikini panties adorned with a delicate white and pink peonies floral pattern, now tragically absorbing the blood that flowed freely from her injury. Her inner thigh was a macabre tapestry, a spiderweb of crimson rivulets weaving across her skin.

"You cut me," Betsy said. The words hung in the air, inadequate for the shock blooming inside her. Her heart thundered against her ribs as she stared at Missy's face. Those familiar features of a shell, combined with the face of a jack-o'-lantern and bloodied knees, now appeared to belong to a stranger, someone unrecognizable. A monster. The pain intensified, a hot, slicing sensation that traveled from her most intimate area down her thigh. Betsy pressed her hand against the wound, feeling warm wetness seep between her fingers, a horrifying acknowledgment of what had just transpired. She couldn't process what had just happened. Missy had cut her. Deliberately. With a scalpel.

Missy slid out from underneath the cubbyhole.

"No need to call Scotland Yard. The case has been solved," Missy said. "You might want to get a pad on that; it looks like you just had an abortion."

"What's wrong with you?" Betsy said. Her voice sounded distant to her own ears, trembling with a mixture of pain, fear, and something else—a deep sense of violation that made her stomach clench. She backed away, her eyes darting back and forth, torn between the cold gaze of Missy and the blood-covered steel blade in her right hand. She glanced behind her, assessing how far she had to go before hitting the wall.

Missy smiled, aware that she had weakened Betsy. However, making Betsy vulnerable was no longer sufficient. Now, she was determined to finish her off just as her father had done with her pet pig, Pinky.

"Why are you doing this?" Betsy said, pressing her left hand against the wound and briefly eyeing the syringe on the desk behind Missy.

"Ethel Wallace tells me you and Jacky boy are a thing and you like to refer to me as thunder thighs behind my back," Missy said.

"That's absurd," Betsy said. "I'm happily married."

"And I believe you," Missy said, her tone insincere. "You do believe me, right?"

Betsy's left hand searched blindly behind her for the axe she had leaned against the wall earlier. She thought about how Missy's transformation from healthcare worker to psycho killer had been swift. She recalled Beth's warning: "John Doe is spreading his evil like wildfire."

Missy stepped forward when Betsy stepped back, but Betsy sensed she was stalling for the right moment to lunge at her.

"Poor Mrs. Shadwack," Missy said.

"Julia?" Betsy said. "What about her?"

"I had to paddle her. She was being bad," Missy said, added humor to her horror.

"You used a defibrillator on Julia?" Betsy said.

"Yeah, and thanks to you, she's dead," Missy said. "You're as worthless as a pecker on an owl."

"Owls have beaks," Betsy said.

Her right hand bumped into the wooden handle. Betsy gripped it just in time to evade Missy's attack, stepping aside as Missy followed through, though she stabbed the wall instead of Betsy's flesh. Betsy came around with the axe blade, slicing through Missy's hand.

Missy screamed, a high-pitched wail that bounced off the walls. Her shriek was one of defeat rather than of pain. Blood spurted from her severed hand, spattering across Missy's orange face and onto the linoleum floor. Betsy gripped the axe handle tighter, her palms slick with her own blood and sweat, her heart hammering against her ribs.

"Well, that's something you don't see every day," Missy said, unfazed by her injury, seemingly immune to pain.

Betsy realized this was no longer the Missy she knew; something else had taken control. While Missy stared at her severed fingers, Betsy seized the opportunity to grab the syringe from the desk and jab it into Missy's buttocks before she could react.

"Here's a little something for your pain," Betsy said as she pushed the plunger, injecting the sedative into Missy, leaving the syringe embedded in her skin.

With her good hand, Missy yanked the syringe from her backside and hurled it at Betsy, who was limping down the hall, leaving a trail of blood. The syringe didn't come close to hitting Betsy.

"By the way, pumpkin head," Betsy said, shouted back to Missy. "Tammy's outfit on you is bursting at the seams."

The nurses' station buzzed with residents needing care. Missy held up her mangled hand, dripping blood from her elbow onto the glowing intercom panel. She examined her injury with fascination.

"You'll have to wait; we're a little short-handed at the moment," she said, rotated her hand from palm to the backside, admired the injury.

CHAPTER 50

As Beth was blessing the entrance of the chapel and herself, Betsy hobbled to her, blood trickling down her right thigh.

"Oh my gosh," Beth said. "Come in and lie down."

Inside the chapel, Betsy settled onto the last pew on the right side, pressing her hand against the wound.

"Beth, I need you to stitch me up," Betsy said.

"I've never done it before," Beth said.

"But you're a nurse, right?" Betsy said.

"Well... not exactly," Beth said. "The nurse's outfit is a costume."

"After all I've seen tonight, why am I not surprised?" Betsy said. "Okay, I'll just have to talk you through it."

"I have an extra pad I got from the restroom," Beth said.

"Perfect, good thinking," Betsy said. "But first, we need a tourniquet."

Initially, Beth considered tearing the hem of her skirt, but then she came up with a better idea. She stood up and took off her bra, using the elastic band to tie it around Betsy's bleeding thigh.

"That will work," Betsy said, retrieving some sterile butterfly stitches from her pocket.

"You usually carry adhesive stitches with you?" Beth said, wanting to keep Betsy talking as she showed signs of losing consciousness.

"Like I told you before," Betsy said, her speech slightly slurred. "As a Boy Scout mom, I've had a lot of training in being prepared."

"That's right, you did say that," Beth said.

Beth closed Betsy's wound, applying butterfly sutures from the top to the bottom until she slowed the bleeding. She placed the menstrual pad over Betsy's stitches.

"Keep pressure on the pad," Beth said to Betsy.

"You said you're not a nurse," Betsy said. "You could've fooled me."

"I did fool you like I fooled everyone else," Beth said, causing Betsy to laughed.

"About the insulin I sent you to get," Betsy said, "did you fumble the ball on purpose? I mean, what was your plan?"

"I have an aunt who was a diabetic," Beth said. "But I was still unsure about doing it right and hoped Cloreese would show up to give me confidence when—" Beth said.

"When what?" Betsy said.

"I heard Jennifer's voice asking me to let her out of the freezer," Beth said.

"That's some freaky, spine-chilling sensation," Betsy said.

"Exactly what I was thinking," Beth said.

"Beth," Betsy said.

"Yeah," Beth said.

"I think John Doe is here because of me," Betsy said.

"Why?" Beth said.

"I cheated death," Betsy said.

"How?" Beth said.

"I was a Jane Doe," Betsy said.

"I'm not following you," Beth said.

"I'm an abortion survivor. An unsuccessful abortion, unnamed, abandoned, unwanted, and left for dead," Betsy said.

"Oh my gosh, Betsy," Beth said, her heart aching. "That's awful having to carry that burden."

"I endured five days of saline infusion and an oxytocin drip which burned my lungs, eyes, and skin. Doctors treated me for respiratory distress syndrome. My mother was thirty-one weeks pregnant with me when the doctor laid me on the table like a piece of meat; I weighed just over two pounds. I was alone. A nurse heard my weak whimper and rushed me to the ICU. Once I fully recovered, a family adopted me," Betsy said. "The abortion doctors labeled me as the dreaded complication. I later found out there's an entire network of abortion survivors."

"I'm so sorry, Betsy, you had to go through that," Beth said.

"This is my body, Beth. Where were my rights?" Betsy said.

"Last year, doctors performed over a million abortions. I looked it up."

"Don't put the blame on yourself," Beth said. "John Doe is evil, and his nature is to kill, steal, and destroy."

"You're going to have to end this fight tonight and stay alive," Betsy said. "You must protect the residents from Missy. Do you understand what that means?"

"I believe I do," Beth said.

"Good," Betsy said. "There's one more thing?"

"What?" Beth said.

"You need to clean up my blood trail in the hallway. Once Missy fully regains consciousness, she'll follow it straight to here."

"Okay," Beth said.

"You need to hurry," Betsy said, her eyelids drooping as she struggled to stay awake. "I don't know how much time you have. Get that bucket from the restroom."

"The one you accused me of throwing my used pad into, as if I thought it was a trash can?" Beth said, recalling the mental image.

"Yes, it was overflowing with blood," Betsy said. "I apologize for being snooty."

"It's fine. I know the one," Beth said.

"Good," Betsy said. "Use a mop to create drips down the hall toward the room where Kate's car crashed; that will lead Missy in the opposite direction from here."

"Got it," Beth said.

"We can only hope that if she enters that room, she finds Moby Dick to keep her occupied," Betsy said.

Beth thought it wasn't a good time to tell Betsy that the bucket overflowing with blood was John Doe playing tricks on her mind. Jennifer had confirmed with the same baffled expression as Beth had when Betsy saw something different from what they witnessed. The water was clear, and the bucket only had about ten percent collected in it. Beth remembered the water was shallow, because it was annoying to her to hear the ping every time a drip hit the bottom of the pail. But now was not the time to argue over who was right. Beth considered whether rusty water from a leaky pipe could trick someone into thinking the spots on the linoleum floor were blood from an injured person rather than rust. However, she agreed that the blood trail leading to the chapel had to be cleaned up. Just as she was about to stand, Betsy grabbed her arm.

"One last thing," Betsy said.

"What?" Beth said.

"Tell my boy and my husband I love them," Betsy said. "You know when you said earlier about intuition?"

"Yes," Beth said.

"Well, I believe my son is still alive," Betsy said.

"I do as well," Beth said. "But you can tell them yourself. I've found a way to stop this evil."

Betsy lost consciousness momentarily before Beth shook her awake.

"Come on, Betsy, stay with me," Beth said. "It's almost morning. The next crew will be coming in soon."

Beth heard a vibration coming from Betsy's pocket. It was Jennifer's phone. A text had come through from Jennifer's boyfriend, the doctor at Lakeside Memorial Hospital:

"Mrs. Rose Windslow is in my care. She's doing well. Tiffany's tomorrow night at around seven works for me. Call me when you get a chance."

"Betsy, Rose isn't dead. John Doe had us believing a lie. That means your son is alive," Beth said with excitement, but Betsy didn't respond.

Beth wasn't sure if Betsy had heard her, but she realized she was no help to Betsy by just sitting there waiting for her to die. She hoped the day shift crew would arrive in time to save Betsy, but until then, she had to keep Missy from finding them.

CHAPTER 51

Beth opened the door to find Missy standing in the hallway, an axe gripped in her good hand. The sight startled Beth.

"Trick or treat," Missy said, a sadistic grin spreading across her face. Beth raised her eyebrows in disgust as she noticed the two severed fingers dangling from Missy's earlobes, attached by paperclips that pierced through the flesh like fishing hooks through worms. No matter which way Missy turned, her fingers pointed in the right direction. Beth thought, and then she considered for a moment how morbid it was for her to reflect on Missy injury that way, but under the circumstances it was awfully amusing.

Beth looked down at Missy's bandaged hand.

"Missy, you're not looking too good," Beth said. "Think you might need stitches."

"Is that the opinion of Beth Meyers pretending to be a nurse, or Ms. Beth Bennett, the time-traveling school teacher?" Missy said. "Oh, that's right you are one-in-the-same."

"Did you come to pray?" Beth said.

"I came to get Betsy," Missy said. "I know she's here."

"Oh, she's here," Beth said. "Come on in." Beth knew that the demon in Missy wouldn't cross over holy ground. To do so would be a contradiction to its nature.

"Bring her to me," Missy said.

"I can ask her, but I doubt she's up to seeing visitors right now," Beth said. "Maybe come back later when you've learned some manners."

"Why don't you look me in the eye when you're talking to me?" Missy said.

"And who would I be looking at? Your name tag reads Tammy, yet you look like Missy. You seem a little old for role-playing. You're not Missy, and you're sure not Tammy. Whoever or whatever you are, you need to return to where you came from and give Missy back her body," Beth said.

"If you don't bring Betsy to me, I'll start killing the residents, starting with your boyfriend Jed," Missy said.

Beth avoided eye contact, looking at the floor, then back to the axe, then from side to side, keeping her awareness busy. Then she looked away from Missy's body for a moment, long enough to notice the font at arm's reach to her right. Lightning struck, dimming the lights. Beth scooped up some holy water in her right hand from the font beside her and flung it in Missy's face.

"Here, you need to cool down," Beth said.

Missy's skin burned, and the pain tormented her. She dropped the axe and clutched her face. The axe head bounced with a loud clang onto the floor. Smoke rose from between Missy's fingers on her good hand. Missy stepped back in agony, as if Beth had thrown acid on her.

Beth gasped at the damage to Missy's complexion, which looked like hot wax melting. She stooped and picked up the axe. As Missy revealed her burning face, Beth swung back and let the weight of the axe head lead the strike, not stopping for anything—especially not flesh or bone. Missy's head came off, spinning a few times before hitting the floor.

Beth recalled Missy's earlier words: 'I had a pet pig I named Pinky. One day when I was at school, my dad cut Pinky's head off…'

Somewhere beyond the walls, a transformer exploded, booming like a cannon shot. The lights in the hallway went out. Missy's glowing red eyes dimmed for a moment before going out. The emergency lights in the ceiling sputtered to life, bathing the hallway in a searing, unearthly glow.

"You can't blame PMS on this one, lady," Beth said, unsure why she said it; adrenaline from fear surged through her, ready for action. After shouting at Missy's lifeless head, she realized she needed to calm down to think with a rational mind. Just as the red glow faded from Missy's eyes, another pair of glowing eyes appeared farther down the hall.

The hallway lights flickered back on, subtle at first, struggling to maintain power and then illuminating to the fullest degree.

Beyond Missy's decapitated head, Beth spotted John Doe in a wheelchair at the end of the hallway, facing her. He appeared as if still in a coma, though now he was looking up with red glowing eyes, his body motionless and his expression still as a corpse—lifeless. She hid the axe behind her, as if caught playing with matches. The wheelchair rolled toward her, leaving fiery tracks from the melting rubber rims. John Doe smoldered, trailing smoke like steam from a train. Initially, Beth thought he was on fire as smoke shadowed him. When the wheelchair's front wheels passed Missy's decapitated head, her hair caught fire. John Doe continued approaching, with minimal movement at first but building momentum. Before he could roll over Beth, she dodged aside. She swung the axe at his head, but an unseen force ripped it from her grip and hurled it to the ground, where it slid twenty feet before stopping. Missy's blood streaked the linoleum from the business end of the axe while scooting over the surface.

Beth reached into her pocket, retrieving Jennifer's saline solution bottle filled with holy water, and laid a stream across the hallway, a line drawn in the sand, one John Doe couldn't cross. Before he could retreat, she made another line behind him, trapping him in the small confined space right in front of the chapel. His body was still, an empty shell of a man. He made no attempt to communicate. He emitted a putrid odor that almost made Beth vomit.

Jed appeared out of nowhere and reached for the wheelchair's handles.

"No, Jed," Beth said, not having enough time to warn him.

Jed's hands burned as he winced in pain, staring at his blistered palms. Beth shot a stream of holy water onto the handlebars.

"Use her shoes," Jed said to Beth, looking down at Missy's feet. "There's no need to operate since she's lost her head." Jed was referring to Missy's initial costume mimicking the Operations game character Cavity Sam.

Beth grabbed Missy's shoes and placed them over the handlebars; the leather protected her hands from the heat. She tried to move the wheelchair, but it felt like the brakes were on, even though they weren't. Jed attempted to help with his shoulder, but his weak knees prevented him from gaining any leverage. Beth yelled out a declaration of exertion.

"Look," Jed said, motioning for Beth to look down the hallway.

It seemed like all the residents crowded the hallway at the same time, with occupants moving in unison in the same direction. What had been empty moments before were now congested. It resembled a cattle call for extermination, like at Jonestown, Guyana, where the mass murder of The Peoples Temple gathered for their fair share of the sweet drink laced with cyanide. Like dazed zombies on a mission, staring forward, all grouped together like an unfit battalion marching to war. Some limped; some were in wheelchairs; others were behind walkers or on crutches; all moving toward them.

Out of Beth's peripheral vision, she saw movement from the opposite direction.

"They're coming at us from both sides," she said.

Jed swiveled his head to glance in the other direction, following Beth's motion.

A lynch mob was advancing at a creeping pace, like puppets controlled by an evil force. Their flaws made the mass sluggish. As they passed each room, landline telephones jumped off their cradles, emitting busy signals that echoed like a fire alarm, growing louder but remaining in unison.

All the lights went out, followed by a thunderclap. Beth and Jed could only make out pairs of red glowing eyes still coming toward them without letting up.

"They have the virus," a man's voice said.

"The unvaccinated are our enemies who walk among us," a female voice said.

"You all are sounding like a coward rock singer speaking out about what he knows nothing about; scared; wetting his pants like some little momma's boy," Jed said.

"I didn't know Hitler could sing," Beth said in a whisper.

The soft emergency lighting came on.

"You're our enemy," the one on crutches said, jabbing one crutch in the air for emphasis.

"We need to burn your bodies," the one in the wheelchair said.

"I want to live," an elderly woman called from the back.

The mob was about to reach Beth and Jed when, to their surprise, Roland emerged from his coma. He charged the wheelchair from behind, hitting it with his shoulder like a football lineman defending the quarterback. With the rosary still around his neck, John Doe had no power over him. The chair began inching forward toward the chapel threshold, even though the wheels weren't rotating, as the rubber rims liquefied like melted wax. Raphael, the cat, leaped onto John Doe's face, hissing and screeching. The brakes felt as though they had released. The cat's desperation to act on impulse was unpredictable—and brave.

The man on crutches grabbed Beth's sleeve, tugging on it and ripping her clothes. She pressed her arm closer against her chest to cover her exposed breasts. Since she had used her bra as a tourniquet for Betsy, she now had no support. Beth's hand clutched at the torn fabric, pulling the edges together where they would meet, fighting against the man on crutches to maintain her modesty.

"Push," Beth yelled.

Roland pushed even harder than he'd thought was possible, exerting himself as though he hadn't been bedridden over the last few months. But just as John Doe reached the invisible line of the threshold that Beth had blessed with holy water, all the busy signals echoing through the hallway ceased, followed by an explosion and a burst of bright light.

Beth thought she saw the daytime crew entering the front door down the hallway, the blinding morning sun behind them, just before the image faded.

CHAPTER 52

Jed lay on the floor when he heard the fire extinguisher discharge. He propped himself up to see Beth extinguishing the flames that were consuming some greasy rags in a large thirty-gallon brown fiber drum. The year is 1966, and they were in the basement of the Weather the Storm Girls' School for the Blind and Deaf. Raphael, the cat, was beside Jed, hissing at the boilers. Both Jed and Beth followed the cat's gaze to a pair of glowing red eyes lurking behind the boiler.

Beth reached for the holy water.

"Hey John," Beth said. "I'm back."

She sprayed the holy water at the glowing eyes, but before the stream could make contact, the eyes flickered out. Not like a candle—but like the filament in a bulb that, once dead, leaves a ghost after-image burned into your retina. John Doe vanished before the water reached him. Where John Doe had been standing, the cinder blocks darkened with moisture. The water splattered against the wall and trickled down to the floor. John Doe was gone.

Raphael remained calm, licking his front paws.

Beth wiped a streak of foam from her sleeve and set the extinguisher upright again.

Jed stood up and moved to Beth's side. His knees felt fine; there were no aches or pains. He was now a year older than Beth, the same year-gap as before, when she'd first disappeared.

The stairwell door banged open, and Roland's footsteps hammered down the stairs in uneven beats. He appeared on the landing halfway down, his eyes wide and wild, and looked down at Beth and Jed, who were kissing.

"Is everyone okay?" Roland said, panting.

Beth smiled and looked at Jed.

"I'm not sure," Beth said. "How does it feel, Jed, to have your life rewind to live all over again?"

"The first time was practice," he said. "This time, I'm going to make it count."

"The storm outside is gone," Roland said. "It just vanished."

"It's all clear down here," Jed said. "Beth put out the fire."

"Okay, I'm going to check on everyone," Roland said, dashing back up the stairs he had just descended.

Beth turned to Jed.

"Yeah, but I feel like another one is starting," Beth said, smiled.

"That's one fire I can live with," Jed said.

They embraced each other.

Epilogue

One Year Later, October 1967

An orange banner arched across the concrete walkway leading to the front entrance of Weather the Storm, the girls' school for the blind and deaf, announcing in block letters: HALLOWEEN FALL FESTIVAL. The school grounds buzzed with vendors and their booths or tables, each offering its own novelty. Vendors hawked jars of preserves and handmade jewelry, while others displayed patchwork quilts, and a local bookseller had set up a bargain bin for well-thumbed romance paperbacks and Gothic horror. The crowd—parents, siblings, teachers, and a few local dignitaries—milled about, craning necks and bumping elbows. This event served as a fundraiser to support upgrades, including a new fire suppression system, alarms, and special alert devices for the deaf, like red flashing lights installed in every classroom.

Raffle tickets were being sold at a booth next to a bake sale, where students showcased brownies, pumpkin bread, cupcakes, and cookies, drawing in passersby. Beth observed that the organizers had positioned the bake sale table near the entrance, ensuring that everyone entering or leaving the event had to walk past it twice. Nearby, people admired the arts and crafts table. Another fundraising event was the Read-a-thon, where donors pledged a dollar for every page read within a two-hour period. Parents enjoyed participating in games adapted for those with visual and hearing impairments, such as tug-of-war, three-legged race, and Sensory Treasure Hunt. Parents and teachers hovered, ready to intervene if a skinned knee or bruised elbow threatened to spoil the day. Meanwhile, the kitchen staff volunteered their time cooking hotdogs and burgers over a wood-burning grill, while teachers supervised students who delighted in crawling and walking through concrete tunnels, sliding down metal slides, and playing on the teeter-totter. Beth noticed the set of wheelchair swings as a recent addition to the playground.

Tammy Proctor, Jennifer O'Toole, and Missy White stood by the dart-and-balloon game. When Beth glanced their way, she saw Jennifer, who was mostly deaf, helping Missy, who had a visual impairment, to throw darts. Tammy laughed when the vendor realized Missy was blind; he stepped aside to stay out of their way. Missy managed to pop a balloon and won a small stuffed giraffe. Just typical fifteen-year-olds, Beth thought. Spotting Beth and Jed walking together along the sidewalk, Tammy waved to them, and Beth waved back. Noticing Tammy's gesture, Jennifer turned to look as well. Taking Missy's hand, Tammy and Jennifer skipped to Beth.

"Mrs. Bennett," Tammy said, using sign language.

"It's Mrs. Myers now," Beth said, correcting Tammy while showing her wedding band on her ring finger.

"Oh, sorry," Tammy said. "Do you mind if we take Missy to play tug-of-war?"

"Missy, the girls want to take you to play tug-of-war. Are you up for it?" Beth said.

Missy nodded.

Beth communicated back to Tammy using hand signals.

"She said yes," Beth said. "That's fine by me."

The girls giggled and turned, skipping away in the direction they had come, with Jennifer and Tammy guiding Missy.

Beth thought it was strange to see these kids, knowing some of them would eventually have grandchildren named after them. She felt fortunate to witness both grandparents and grandchildren in such a brief span of time. Tammy Proctor's granddaughter would become Tammy Bisset, Jennifer O'Toole's granddaughter would be Jennifer Givings, and Missy White's granddaughter would be Missy Crenshaw. It occurred to her that names weren't just labels; sometimes they were seeds, planted and waiting to sprout in another lifetime.

Jed squeezed her hand as they wandered away from the noise. Beth was showing, but only a little—a modest bump beneath her pink sweater. She admired how her wedding ring sparkled in the sunlight. The sky was clear, providing a beautiful blue backdrop.

"The doctor said I'm due on February 29th," Beth said. "So, every four years, our daughter gets a real birthday."

"I thought February only had 28 days," Jed said.

"Next year is a leap year," Beth said.

"Oh, right," Jed said.

Beth stopped without warning, while Jed's stride to another step ahead, losing his hold on Beth's right hand and spilling cider from the paper cup he was holding.

"Are you okay?" Jed said.

Beth placed her right hand on her belly.

"The baby just kicked," she said. "Here."

She guided Jed's hand to the same spot on her belly.

"I feel it," Jed said.

Out of the corner of her eye, she noticed a billboard across the street, advertising the proposed design for a new nursing home.

Roland was talking with a man surveying the land when he noticed Beth and Jed. He waved first, then made an exaggerated jog across the street, dodging an oncoming orange Volkswagen Beetle to reach them.

Beth gasped, initially mistaking the orange Volkswagen Beetle for an orange AMC Gremlin, the car that Kate drove. The color was very similar. Once she realized her mistake, she regained her calmness with no one noticing.

Meanwhile, Jed focused on Roland crossing the street.

"Hey, congratulations on the wedding!" Roland called out as he approached, slightly out of breath.

"Thank you," Beth and Jed both said, their voices overlapping.

"When's the baby due?" Roland said.

"February 29th," Beth said, smiled.

"February is when they're breaking ground on the new nursing home over there," Roland said, gesturing behind him.

"Hopefully, my baby jumping for the first time, just now, is a good omen," Beth said.

"Really?" Roland said.

"I felt it," Jed said.

"Have you decided on a name?" Roland said.

"Her name will be Betsy," Beth said.

"That's nice," Roland said. "But doesn't February only have 28 days?"

"1968 is leap year," Jed said proudly, having just learned this.

"Oh, that's right," Roland said.

"Judging from the billboard picture, the building looks very nice," Beth said.

"Oh, yes," Roland said, then glanced down at the sidewalk, appearing troubled.

"Is something wrong?" Beth said.

"It's just that this nursing home is privately owned," Roland said.

"Is that a bad thing?" Jed said.

"No, I'm not implying that," Roland said. "Many privately owned nursing homes provide quality care."

"Based on the picture, it seems a lot of money is going into its construction," Jed said.

"Yes," Roland said. "The owner has plenty of funds and isn't taking shortcuts."

"I bet the chapel will be big and beautiful," Beth said.

"Well," Roland said, hesitating.

"What? There's no chapel?" Jed said.

"Right," Roland said.

"No chapel in a nursing home?" Jed said, surprised.

"You've got to be kidding," Beth said in disbelief.

"I wish I were," Roland said. "The owner specifically requested no chapel."

"Who is the owner, John Doe?" Beth said.

Both Jed and Roland looked at Beth.

Roland shrugged.

"Let's hope history doesn't repeat itself in this case," Jed said.

"Don't you mean the future?" Roland said.

"It baffles the mind if you give it too much thought," Jed said.

"I'll teach Betsy the proverb: hope for the best but prepare for the worst," Beth said. "If John Doe returns, the family will be ready."

Beth paused, envisioning herself and Jed in wheelchairs at the new nursing home, holding hands and watching children play in the schoolyard across the street. Behind them, the illuminated exit sign flickered on and off and then went out completely.

THE END

Acknowledgement

Someone always seems genuinely curious about what inspired me to write a story. To those with a knack for knowing, this is for you. One day, I received a phone call from my dad, who cried on the other end. This struck me as odd; it marked the first time I ever heard my dad bawling. When I asked him what was wrong, he said the nursing home had just called and told him, "Your wife is dead," before hanging up on him. He sounded frantic, to say the least. I couldn't believe what I heard. How could anyone be so cold and insensitive, I thought. I tried to comfort him and calm him down. Later, I discovered that the nurse who called my dad rushed to leave since her shift had ended. So, if you recall the part in the story where Kate calls Rose Windslow's husband to inform him of his wife's death, followed by her slamming the phone onto the cradle, that mirrors what happened to my dad.

Sign up for the newsletter at:
pl.bookinfo.newsletter@gmail.com
to receive updates about the release of my next book.

Share this link with a friend to obtain their copy of LAST STOP.

For the author's bio.

HAPPY HAUNTING!

Made in United States
Orlando, FL
09 December 2025